D0374110

HISTORICAL WHODUNITS

Hy Conrad

ILLUSTRATED BY
Julie Collins Rousseau

STERLING PUBLISHING CO., INC.

New York

To Jeanette,
Everything a good editor should be

EDITED BY Jeanette Green
DESIGNED BY Richard Oriolo

LIBRARY OF CONGRESS CATALOGING-IN-PUBLICATION DATA

Conrad, Hy.
  Historical whodunits / Hy Conrad ; illustrated by Julie Collins
  Rousseau.
    p. cm.
  Includes bibliographical references and index.
  ISBN 1-4027-2172-2
1. Puzzles. 2. Detective and mystery stories. I. Title.

GV1507.D4C6672 2005
793.73--dc22

2005013607

2   4   6   8   10   9   7   5   3

Published by Sterling Publishing Co., Inc.
387 Park Avenue South, New York, NY 10016
© 2005 by Hy Conrad
Distributed in Canada by Sterling Publishing
c/o Canadian Manda Group, 165 Dufferin Street
Toronto, Ontario, Canada M6K 3H6
Distributed in Great Britain by Chrysalis Books Group PLC
The Chrysalis Building, Bramley Road, London W10 6SP, England
Distributed in Australia by Capricorn Link (Australia) Pty. Ltd.
P.O. Box 704, Windsor, NSW 2756, Australia

Manufactured in the United States of America
All rights reserved

Sterling ISBN 1-4027-2172-2

For information about custom editions, special sales, premium and
corporate purchases, please contact Sterling Special Sales
Department at 800-805-5489 or specialsales@sterlingpub.com.

CONTENTS

INTRODUCTION

IN THE WORLD OF MYSTERY fiction, ancient detectives are popular heroes. But historians—killjoys that they are— tell us that no such creatures existed. No wise monks roamed the European countryside solving murders. No clever Roman soldier pieced together clues to the mysterious death of a senator.

We, as modern humans, assume that the physical world is ruled by cause and effect. But in a long-ago age dominated by the weird and inexplicable, from spontaneous combustion to random disease, the notion that footprints might lead to a killer probably made less sense than a dream from God telling you whom to arrest. Crime, the historians say, was generally solved by eyewitnesses, confessions (often extracted by torture), and supernatural explanations.

And yet, I'd like to think that every now and then some exceptional ancient must have viewed the evidence and come to an epiphany. Surely a Chinese bureaucrat or Egyptian official saw the lack of blood around a wound and realized that the victim had been dead before he'd been stabbed. And if this isn't the way it was, it's certainly the way I choose to envision it.

Now may be a good time to admit that I'm not a slave to accuracy. I and my fellow TV scribes ignore the truth on a regular basis. In the mythical land of *CSI,* the geeks who process lab tests can be found following leads, brandishing weapons, and grilling suspects. In my own land of *Monk,* an alarming number of men kill their wives, and a body can be balanced on the minute hand of a clock tower. You might watch our shows and reasonably conclude that we're dumber than bricks. We're not. We're just a little more willing than bricks to stretch the facts for the sake of a good yarn.

Having said that, I must now ask you to believe that within these pages I've tried to be historically true. I really have. Detectives may not have existed, but I'd like to think that I've gotten the other details right. From the layout of a Roman villa to the politics of a Swiss hamlet, I've done my share of research. For me, that was half the challenge. The other half was to make these whodunits fair and solvable. Again, I tried.

So…good luck, have fun, and if you come upon some glaring inaccuracy, you will at least have the satisfaction of knowing I'm genetically closer to a brick than you.

—HY CONRAD

MYSTERIES

FALL OF A
SOCIAL CLIMBER

Rome, 220 A.D.

MODERATUS SCRAPED HIS MASTER'S BACK and idly dreamed of the day when he could buy his freedom. The coins were coming in slowly, one or two on the festival of Saturnalia, perhaps an unexpected one if Marcus Livius was in a good mood. Right now, Marcus Livius was not in a good mood.

They were in the grand baths, newly completed by the Emperor Caracalla. They sat in the warm room, the slaves using strigils to scrape olive oil, and the dirt it trapped, off their owners' bodies. The Roman elite came to this ornate complex several times a week, to soak and steam and gossip and gamble. Moderatus continued to work on Marcus Livius, while his friend Norteo, a Nubian from North Africa, scraped Achilius, Marcus's son. As usual, the men spoke as if their slaves had no ears.

"You were schooled for a life in government," said Marcus, anger rising in his voice, "and, by Jove, you will do it. You are a member of my household, my property." That was true enough. Marcus had the power of life and death over all who lived under his roof. But Achilius was no longer a child.

"There is nothing ignoble in designing monuments and buildings," he begged his father. "The man who built the Coliseum was of the senator class."

"But that was his passion, not his trade. Building is best learned in the lower ranks of the army. Our family has worked too long to take such a step backwards."

Moderatus nodded unconsciously in agreement. No citizen of the equestrian class was more status conscious than Marcus Livius. He wore a trim on his toga that was nearly purple, a color reserved for the clothes of emperors and the trim of senators. He spent lavishly to entertain his betters. And when they wouldn't accept his dinner invitations, he would invite poets and actors—talented, famous men, but on the scandalous margin of good society—to dine at the house of Livius.

Marcus dismissed his son's plea and once more turned his attention to today's dinner party. "It's quite a coup having Eppides the Greek as our guest."

"Will he be the entertainment?" asked Achilius with a half-hidden smirk.

Marcus Livius was shocked. "Eppides is the greatest actor in Rome."

"He plays the women's roles in comedies," replied Achilius.

Eppides did indeed play the female roles, but to such great acclaim. He was a recent arrival from Athens, historic home of the arts, where he was reputed to be a living legend.

"Eppides is a legend," Marcus Livius said, echoing the common sentiment. "He is never seen in public, not even at the baths, and almost never accepts invitations. He will share my dining couch. I would not insult him by asking him to perform. There will be the lute and pipes and a troupe of dancers."

It was early afternoon when the Livius men and their slaves arrived home from the baths. Moderatus and Norteo made their masters comfortable in the coolness of the atrium, then wandered off to the kitchen where Sabbina Livius, the matriarch, was busy supervising the upcoming meal. The daily fare was usually modest, fishbone soup or dormouse cooked in honey. But for a dinner party, there would be no expense spared. Songbirds were being de-boned and dressed to look like fish. Young beef was being blanched and molded to look like songbirds. To disguise food as other food was the height of fashion—and the slave Norteo was especially skilled at it.

"Norteo!" The Lady Sabbina saw him enter and practically screamed his name. "What can I do? The monger sold my stupid cook a fish that is on the point of spoiling..."

Norteo hurried to the spice cabinet, lifting down the small clay containers of dried herbs. "Never worry," he reassured her. "I will make some garum, a strong sauce to disguise the taste."

The lady of the house sighed and smiled. "If you make this meal succeed, I will buy your freedom myself. I swear. This time I will."

Moderatus felt bad for his friend. For two previous dinner feasts, a desperate Sabbina had promised Norteo his freedom, just like this. On both occasions he had triumphed and on both occasions, Marcus Livius had taken the money, refused to let him go, and beaten both the slave and his wife when they objected.

"I know you mean it," Norteo said softly as he mixed the spices with olive oil and wine from a small clay amphora. "But for as long as your husband lives, there will be freedom for neither one of us."

Moderatus expected such a comment, even if whispered, to earn the Nubian slave a beating, or at the least a hard slap. But Lady Sabbina only shook her head sadly, as if to agree.

Moderatus left the kitchen. He was sweeping out the front foyer when a shadow fell across the threshold and a short, slim man walked in. In the shade of the wall, Moderatus almost mistook him for a woman. The man carried himself regally, despite his attire—a modest, everyday tunic and a bundle tucked under his arm. Without a word spoken, Moderatus knew his identity.

"The home of Marcus Livius?" asked the actor Eppides, today's guest of honor.

Moderatus bowed. But before he could even get out a word

of greeting, the master of the house was scurrying over from his cushioned bench. "Dear Eppides, we are honored," he said with a bow much too low for his station. "Forgive us for not being prepared, but..."

"I am early," the actor said with an ingratiating smile. "I was hoping to impose on your hospitality. I hear your home is one of the few to contain a private bath."

Moderatus realized that the bundle must contain the actor's dinner robes, plus a strigil for cleaning and a razor for shaving.

"I would be honored to have you use my bath," Marcus Livius said. "It is in my private quarters."

"I have never enjoyed bathing in public," Eppides explained as they walked off together. "Off the stage, I am somewhat of a recluse."

Marcus Livius rallied the servants to prepare the room. Screens were erected for absolute privacy. Water was heated and the finest oils laid out. Toward the end of the bath, Marcus himself intruded on the actor, trespassing behind the screen to offer fresh, warm towels.

The other guests arrived at the regular mid-afternoon hour. To take advantage of the fine weather, Sabbina Livius had transformed the peristyle, the rear garden, into a dining room, lining the dining couches around the small tables that would hold the food. In the center, a wooden platform had been placed on the ground, a stage for the entertainment.

Moderatus and the other slaves were kept busy serving the meal. Norteo the Nubian was assigned to filling the finger bowls in which the diners would wash their greasy hands. True to his word, Marcus Livius shared his couch and bowl with the famed actor. As the day slipped slowly into evening, the torches were lit and the feast held all the promise of a huge success. A general of the second legion vigorously praised the elaborate dishes, and not one of the senators fell asleep during the epic poem honoring the last emperor.

As always, Lady Sabbina occupied the couch closest to the

kitchen, a perfect position for a hostess. A pair of slaves carried in a platter of peacock breasts and she carefully inspected it, taking a few extra seconds to rearrange the peacock feathers decorating the edges.

Achilius, the family's only son, shared a couch with two of his friends. Typical of the youths of the day, they whispered among themselves, ignoring the poets and making eyes at the female dancers. Moderatus handed a jug to Achilius and noticed how little water the young man added to his wine before passing the jug to his father at the next couch.

Marcus Livius diluted his cup in the accepted fashion. But even weak wine can intoxicate. The honeyed concoction, combined with the success of his party, had put Marcus in an expansive mood. "These poets and dancers are good enough," he slurred to his guests. "But we must impose upon the incomparable Eppides to honor us with an example of his skill. Perhaps a scene from Plautus?"

The diners all turned on their couches, expectantly. Moderatus didn't know what to expect. To ask a dinner guest to perform was unheard of.

Eppides paused. A moment later he smiled graciously and rose to his feet. Applause greeted him as he stepped up on the wooden platform. The garden fell into a hushed silence, broken only by the labored breathing of the host. This lone sound only grew more intense, until Marcus Livius was stumbling to his feet, knocking over the finger bowl in front of him.

All of Rome knew what the effects of poison looked like. For hundreds of years, poison had been the empire's favorite means of dispatching relatives and enemies. It could be taken from the cheery, yellow buttercup or from the roots of the autumn crocus. Hemlock disguised in honey had killed the famed Seneca. But to be poisoned at the feast table, where so much of the food was eaten communally, that was unusual.

Moderatus watched from a distance as a general and a senator rushed to the rich man's side, eased him to the ground and tried to make him comfortable. If Marcus Livius knew the identity of his poisoner, he didn't use his last gasps of breath to say. Sabbina and Achilius were on their feet, saying nothing, while the dying man's favorite hound lapped calmly at the puddle left from the spilled finger bowl.

It was hours later, after the guests had rushed home to spread the scandalous news, that order began to be restored. Sabbina Livius had the body placed in the dining room and the house draped in mourning. Moderatus had joined the other slaves in cleaning up the rear garden when Achilius called his name and took him aside.

"I've been watching you," the son said, his tone somber. "You're a clever man—and you see things. Tell me, Moderatus, how much do you want your freedom?"

In a matter of minutes the deal was struck. Moderatus would try to discover the truth. And if he could prove to the world that someone other than Achilius was responsible for his father's death, then Achilius would buy the slave his freedom.

(1) Who poisoned Marcus Livius? (2) How did the poisoning occur? (3) What was the motive?

If you've already solved this mystery, check the Solution on p. 130.
To discover additional clues, turn to Gathering Evidence on p. 106.

HISTORICAL NOTES ON ANCIENT ROME

THE STORY OF Rome began around 750 B.C. when the city was founded and ruled by Etruscan kings. When the last king was ousted, Rome became a republic, governed by the rich, high-ranking senators. Rome expanded and prospered, until it was invaded by Hannibal, a general from North Africa, who brought his armies, including war elephants, into Spain and across the Alps. The war was devastating. But at the end, with Hannibal defeated, Rome suddenly found itself with new territories, and an appetite for even more.

Generals became powerful heroes, until the most powerful of all, Julius Caesar, declared himself dictator. He was promptly assassinated for his ambition, but in the chaos that followed, his adopted son, Augustus, took control and became Rome's first emperor, leaving the senate with limited power.

Soon Rome controlled most of the known world, building a system of roads to connect its vast conquests and ushering Europe into its first prolonged peace, the *Pax Romana*.

But the world was changing. Power, trade, and money were moving farther east, and eventually the empire had two capitals, one in Rome and the other in Constantinople. The eastern capital grew in power while Rome in the west became more and more vulnerable to barbarian tribes coming down from Germany.

Rome fell to the barbarians in 410 A.D., but the Roman Empire didn't die. The eastern half, dubbed the Byzantine Empire, thrived for another millennium, until the Ottoman Turks invaded Constantinople and changed its name to Istanbul.

The period from the birth of Rome until the death of the empire encompassed 2,300 years, quite a respectable run in anybody's book.

THE CHALICE
OF CANA

Medieval France, circa 1300

I T WAS A WONDROUS DAY when construction finally resumed on the town's pride and glory—its gift to God, main tourist attraction, largest building, largest employer, and the one thing that could catapult it to the forefront of all French market towns: its cathedral.

Seven winters before, the local chapter's purse had gone empty and a halt was put to the work. But Bishop Faisant was an enterprising soul and responded to this plight in an inspired way. He took the crypt, the first part of the cathedral to be finished, and opened it to the public. The finger bones of John the Baptist and the chalice of Cana were placed on display there, and the response was immediate. Well-paying pilgrims came from all over France and beyond to kiss these relics and pray for miracles.

And now, after seven years of saving every sou, after seven years of watching other towns come closer and closer to completing their own cathedrals, everyone in the ambitious market town was overjoyed to see the returning legions of stonecutters and masons crowding into the cathedral square and reopening their workshops.

Jean Blacksmith stood at his forge as a parade of oxen-pulled carts passed by, buckling under the weight of freshly quarried limestone. There was almost a carnival atmosphere to the holy enterprise, he thought. And he smiled.

Jean's grandfather had been the master smithy here when the foundation stone was laid half a century before. Jean, a young man, had every reason to hope that he himself would still be alive to witness the first holy mass in the monumental house of worship.

At the nearby docks, Bishop Faisant and his assistants were overseeing the unloading of sixty-foot roof beams that had been shipped from the land of Scandinavia. Here, as elsewhere, the cathedral's master architect had been ordained a bishop. What better way to see that the edifice was erected according to God's great plan.

"A glorious day, brother Jean."

Jean waved to the man in the brown robe. Friar Germain was kindly and stout, an elderly member of the Bishop's household. "Indeed glorious," Jean replied. A single raindrop touched his nose, signaling the approach of a spring storm.

At the workshop next to Jean's, doors flew open, startling the timid friar. It was a chill morning, but Robert the glassmaker was already sweating from the heat of his fire. The short, barrel-chested man hailed the smithy and the friar and then asked the smithy how big his workload might be. "My blowing pipe has a hole that won't stay plugged. If you have the time..."

Jean nodded. "I can make you another."

"Good. If we're to have a rose window to outshine the wonder at Rouen..." The glassmaker broke into a mischievous grin. "Look at this." He opened his pouch and poured out a handful of sparkling light. "Imagine the sun coming through these colors."

Jean inspected the finely cut bits of glass and had to agree. He had never seen glass with this kind of brilliance. "Truly, they rival any gems in the Bishop's palace."

"I shall be the judge of that," came a new, deep-throated voice.

Jean glanced behind him and was surprised to see Pierre of Chantilly. A decade earlier, Pierre, a master goldsmith, had been employed here, constructing the gilded and jeweled container that held the ancient wooden chalice believed to have been used by our Lord at the wedding feast of Cana. From here, Pierre had gone to find work at Bayeux.

A few years later, a fire destroyed much of Bayeux's cathedral, and there was a scandalous story—there were always such stories—that the gold of Bayeux's relics had melted into impure puddles, more dross than gold. Pierre fled Bayeux, or so the story went, just one step ahead of the Bishop's men.

The rumors must be false, Jean thought, for Pierre was back here, as boastful and brazen as ever, to work once again on their cathedral's treasures.

Pierre admired the bits of colored glass, then returned them to Robert. "Your work is too good to waste on windows," he said, half chidingly.

Friar Germain was aghast. "Too good for the Lord's windows?" Before he could say more, fat drops of rain began pelting the square. "Oh, dear," he sighed. "The Bishop wants the treasury lit and prepared for visitors. I thought I had hours yet, but this rain will speed up their plans, I'm sure." Germain brought a long wooden key from beneath the folds of his robe. "Excuse me, kind sirs. Duty calls."

From the shelter of the smithy workshop, the three men watched the portly friar puff his way across the square toward the treasury, a single-storied stone hall connected to the rear of the half-built cathedral.

The downpour was quickly sweeping the square clear of the bustling throng.

Robert raised his hood and prepared to brave the pelting drops. "I must get my beechwood logs out of the rain," he said. "Or I won't have ashes to mix with the sand." The ingredients for glass were simple and well known, although every glassmaker had his own secrets.

As soon as Robert disappeared around the edge of his workshop, Pierre also took his leave. With a sigh, Jean returned to his forge, keeping an eye on the worsening weather.

The storm was at its height when a deafening bolt of lightning hit the cathedral. Instantly, the spire towering above the one completed section of roof caught fire. A gash in the lead shell exposed the wooden under-structure and the town watched helplessly as the flaming steeple collapsed, falling into the square and onto the treasury roof.

Jean thanked God for the torrential rain. It did a fair job of dousing the fire. Dozens of workmen ran to the section of fallen spire in the square, smothering the flames with burlap and anything else handy. Several tried to open the treasury door, only to find it locked. "Enter from the cathedral," someone shouted. But this proved impossible, due to a wall of stone that was being stored against the door. "Get the Bishop," someone else shouted.

One of the stonecutters—Jean recognized him as young Louis—mounted the apse scaffolding, climbed like a squirrel, and swung himself onto the treasury roof. The town watched breathlessly. "Very little fire," he shouted down to the thankful crowd. Then young Louis disappeared from view behind the black, broken spire. Seconds later, he reemerged, looking pale and stricken.

The storm had nearly passed now, leaving only a soft sprinkling of mist. "The roof is broken through," Louis shouted. "I looked into the treasury. There's a friar inside. He's..." The man's voice quavered. "He's dead."

In more cases than not, a lightning strike would have set the whole roof ablaze. The heat would have cracked the stone walls and sent decades of work crumbling to the ground. In that sense, the town had been lucky. The spire could be rebuilt in perhaps six months.

But no one felt lucky.

Minutes after Louis had shouted down the news, the Bishop's men broke through the treasury's bolted door. The interior was illuminated by patches of colored light from the narrow windows and by daylight through the hole in the roof. Kindly old Friar Germain lay in the middle of the single room, a knife imbedded in his stomach. And the chalice of Cana, the gilded, bejeweled pride of Normandy, was missing from its place of honor.

Jean and his friends sat by the cold forge, mourning the loss and marveling over the impossibilities. "The only way into the treasury was through the door from the square," concluded Pierre the goldsmith. "And that was bolted from inside. Did Friar Germain let anyone into the treasury with him?"

"No one recalls," said Robert the glassmaker. "I myself went back around my workshop to the stack of beechwood. My apprentice had already covered it with an oilcloth. We stood together under the rear awning until we heard the shouting."

Jean knew Robert's apprentice, an unctuous boy of thirteen with a passion for glassmaking. He would say or do anything to further his life in the craft.

"That chalice was my masterpiece," moaned Pierre. "Generations of pilgrims would have come on their knees and been overwhelmed. Now it's gone. Some greedy fool will melt the gold and sell the jewels."

Jean eyed the goldsmith darkly. Perhaps some greedy fool had committed an even worse sin. Perhaps he had crafted a chalice of impure gold and glass jewels. It would be worth the fool's while to steal back such a fraud, before the forgery could be found out.

"You left here to go to the Bishop's palace?" Jean asked cautiously.

The goldsmith nodded. "We had an appointment to discuss the gold pieces for the altar. I waited for him under the yew tree by the palace doors, trying to stay dry. I didn't hear of the disaster until after the rain stopped." Pierre's nervous hands played with a pair of silver coins. "Perhaps it is the work of Beelzebub, jealous of our devotion. The demon strikes the cathedral, murders a friar, and then steals the Lord's chalice."

"Perhaps," Jean replied. But he suspected otherwise. Curiosity had always been his failing. In an age of faith, curiosity was a dangerous thing, sometimes even deadly. In an hour they would all be blaming the Devil. In a week, this would be the gospel truth, told in song and spoken in ballad.

All the same, the master smithy suspected a more earthly explanation.

(1) Who stabbed Friar Germain? (2) How did the culprit escape detection? (3) What was the motive?

If you've already solved this mystery, check the Solution on p. 131. To discover additional clues, turn to Gathering Evidence on p. 107.

HISTORICAL NOTES ON CATHEDRAL CONSTRUCTION

FROM THE BEGINNING of the Christian era, the building of churches was a vital element in European life. For centuries, Romanesque architecture was the dominant style. Based on ancient Roman construction principles, the resulting buildings featured round arches and massively thick walls.

The building of a new east end of the Cathedral of St. Denis, just outside Paris, heralded a new era. Advances of this period—the pointed arch, the ribbed vault, the flying buttress—made it possible to build taller than ever before, with fewer interior supports. A few years later, these innovations came to Paris and the cathedral of Notre Dame became a benchmark of the new style.

With the advent of this Gothic style of architecture (1150–1550), the obsession with building monumental houses of worship reached a new level. For 400 years, the towns and cities of Europe vied to build the tallest, longest, most impressive cathedrals.

Civic pride fueled this competition. Local merchants and guilds (trade unions) gave generously to each town's efforts, while peasants volunteered their labor in exchange for blessings and indulgences. Teams of trained craftsmen went from town to town, contributing their specialty and then moving on to the next. A cathedral could take anywhere from twenty to a hundred years to complete, depending on financing, politics, and disasters, both natural and architectural. The actual construction was presided over by a chapter, a group of clergymen who, along with the bishop, made all the decisions.

Economics also played a role in these cathedral competitions. An obscure market town could become a bustling center of commerce due to a tall spire, a beautiful window, or some other ornament to attract visitors and pilgrims.

Constructional innovations thrived and were eagerly stolen and adapted, giving the world architectural advances that remained unmatched until the advent of the skyscraper.

Changing tastes and the upheaval of the Reformation brought an end to the era of great cathedrals. The name Gothic wasn't coined until the 17th century to describe this old style that seemed, by then, primitive and barbaric.

Gothic architecture continues to inspire. The Cathedral of St. John the Divine in New York City, the largest Gothic structure in the world, was begun in 1892. Construction was halted in 1941, re-started in 1972 and halted again in 1997. At this point, over a century after its cornerstone was laid, the Cathedral of St. John the Divine remains unfinished.

DEAD MAN'S CHEST

Jamaica, 1690

A LEEWARD BREEZE BLEW *FORTUNE'S DOG* toward the green bay, easily visible on the darkening horizon. There was no boarding party standing along the gunnels and brandishing their weapons, for their goal tonight was not a merchant ship. It was the safety of Port Royal, a British town that welcomed the British pirates.

John Leftum was in his cramped quarters, sorting through a medicine cabinet just plundered from a treasure ship. The riches found on these Spanish galleons had dwindled in recent years, just as their plunder of the American natives had also dwindled. But it was still a worthy prize. Being the ship surgeon, John received one and a quarter shares of the treasure, more than a sailor's but half of the captain's. One of the crew, Old Jacob, had lost a hand in the encounter and so was entitled to a bonus.

As ships go, the *Dog* was a happy one. Will Wesley was a popular captain, elected two years earlier by a vote. But Captain Will had been in a black mood for the past few days, odd behavior for him. He was probably as eager as the crew to reach port and engage in activities forbidden onboard, smoking and gambling and, of course, female companionship.

An hour later, they had careened the pirate ketch on a stretch of beach and were heading into Port Royal, leaving a few guards behind for security. Tomorrow they would begin the onerous task of scraping the bottom of seaweed and barnacles, to keep *Fortune's Dog* as fast as possible. But tonight would be devoted to celebrating their return.

The crew spread throughout the town, heading to their familiar haunts. The largest group, including the captain, his mate Bart Pyle, and the surgeon, sought out The Red Rooster, a tavern owned by Thomas Rooster, one of the rarest creatures in the Caribbean, a retired pirate.

Rooster met them at the tavern door. "I heard you was landed," he said in a cordial growl. "Welcome home." He ushered them inside, but John noticed he didn't touch the brim of his cap, a traditional salute to a captain, pirate or otherwise. Rooster himself had been a captain and Wesley had been his mate. Rumor had it that there was animosity between them, dating back to the days of high plunder ten years before, but neither man ever spoke of it.

They settled in for a night of drinking and gambling and a meal of fresh roast pig, served up by a slave girl Rooster had bought from a sugar plantation. The rest of the serving was done by Martha, the tavern owner's daughter. Out of fear of Rooster, the pirates kept their hands to themselves. But John and Martha shared doe-eyed glances whenever they could. For over the past few months, the surgeon and Martha had fallen in love.

"I'm heading back to the ship," Captain Will said, as he wiped the pig grease from his chin.

"No, stay," said Bart Pyle as he handed Wesley another tankard of rum. "Tell us stories of the old days when the Spanish gold flowed like wine. Let us poor boys drink your health again."

Will Wesley downed the rum in a single, long draught but refused to stay. "You're the heart of the ship, my lads," he said to the dozen or so men. "I'm certain you'll have much more to talk about if I'm not here."

Rooster walked the captain to the door. They shared a few solemn words. Then with a scowl, the captain strode off, never to be seen alive again.

Old Jacob was in his cups that night, more than the others. A round of grapeshot had gone through his left hand during the skirmish for the galleon. Surgeon John had sawed it off at the wrist and the stub seemed free of infection, a small miracle. In a few weeks, he would fit it with a claw. Old Jacob seemed to take his misfortune well enough, except when he had too much to drink.

"It's all Wesley's fault," he muttered a few seconds after the captain had left. "We shouldn't be having to fight. Back in the day of Morgan, they feared us. We raised the flag and they knew to surrender or else. You didn't just kill 'em. They tried to resist and you tortured 'em without mercy. Wesley is too kind a soul. And I don't care who knows it."

Bart Pyle nodded. "But he's still a man to be feared. Unless we're willing to vote him away—and you know it would be unwise to have an angry ex-captain onboard—then we've got to abide by his methods. Barkeep?" he asked, rousing Rooster from his stance by the door. "Have I permission to go after a keg of your best ale?"

Rooster nodded and Pyle disappeared into the storeroom to fetch it.

The evening lasted a few more hours, with Pyle and Rooster both making trips for more ale. John was the only one sober enough to point the way back to the cove. In the tavern, he had alternated his ale with water. Fresh drinking water was a treat for him, since on the ship, it spoiled easily. Rum and beer were the liquid mainstays. He felt as though he had not been fully sober in weeks.

John made sure there were no unconscious mates lurking under the tables and then said his good-byes to Martha. She blushed and squeezed his hand, then closed the heavy door on him and the others. John could hear it being bolted from the inside.

For most of the crew, the next morning dawned in a haze. Since the ship was on its side, the crew had camped out under the palms. It took John a while to realize that the captain was missing. He checked with last night's guards, but they had been drinking from the grog barrel and couldn't recall if Wesley had returned or not.

John gathered a few of the revelers and they wandered back into Port Royal. They divided into groups, with John and Old Jacob returning to the place where they'd last seen their captain. John pounded on the thick tavern door and a minute later heard the bolt slide back. The door opened and there stood Thomas Rooster, his red hair still matted from sleep.

"What do you want?" he asked with a yawn.

John explained about the missing captain. "I'm thinking maybe he came back after we left. Is he here?"

"No." Rooster remained in the doorway, refusing to step aside. "Martha bolted the door last night. The only other door to the outside is in the storeroom and that's always bolted."

By this time, Martha had come down the stairs, clutching her robe at her throat. "Get back to your room," Rooster told his daughter.

She turned around obediently. But something had caught her eye inside the doorway to the storeroom. Martha stepped tentatively toward it. John could hear the lid to a chest creak slowly open. A second later, he heard a scream.

John, Old Jacob, and Rooster ran to the storeroom. On the floor, just inside the door, was a Spanish money chest, a memento from the old days. Seeping out of a bottom corner was a pool of clotting blood. And inside.... Inside lay the body of Captain Will Wesley, stabbed through the heart with a small, thin dagger.

"My father didn't kill him," Martha pleaded to her friend. "Last night, after bolting the door, we put the tankards back on the shelf, then went up to our quarters."

John wanted to believe her and Rooster did indeed deny the deed. But no one else could have done it. "Both the front and storeroom doors were bolted. How could Captain Will have come back without you or your father letting him in?"

"I don't know," said Martha. "Johnny, my love, the governor will try him for murder."

"That won't happen," said John, and it was true. His fellow pirates, under the leadership of Pyle, were even now planning to hang her father without any trial. But this he didn't say.

"The common thought is that Captain Will came back. The two men fought. Rooster put the body in the chest to keep it from your sight until he could dispose of it."

"That's not true. Father did not go down again until you knocked. The stairs creak massively. I would have heard."

"I'll try to fathom what happened," the young surgeon promised.

(1) Who killed Captain Will Wesley? (2) How was it done? (3) What was the motive?

If you've already solved this mystery, check the Solution on p. 132.
To discover additional clues, turn to Gathering Evidence on p. 108.

HISTORICAL NOTES ON THE AGE OF PIRATES

ALMOST AS SOON as men began transporting valuables on the sea, other men went sailing off to rob them. Early pirates plied the Aegean Sea over three thousand years ago, robbing Phoenician traders, raiding unprotected coastal villages, and kidnapping wealthy citizens for ransom.

The Scandinavian Vikings of the ninth century were essentially a tribe of pirates, swooping in on their fast longboats and striking terror into the coastal regions of Europe.

A few centuries later, Islamic pirates began a long tradition of raiding Christian ships in the Mediterranean. Unable to stop them, many countries, including a young United States, paid these Barbary pirates not to attack their vessels. One of the first actions of the United States Marines was to defeat the pirates at Tripoli in 1805, a battle memorialized in the Marine hymn ("to the shores of Tripoli").

Soon after the Spanish discovered the riches of the Americas, pirates from other countries began raiding their treasure ships. Some of these pirate crews were actually in the employ of European governments. Called privateers, they were commissioned by their kings to plunder enemy ships. Sir Walter Raleigh was one such crown-approved pirate.

Pirates continued to skirt the boundaries between legal and illegal status, with one ex-pirate, Henry Morgan, becoming Governor of Jamaica, and another, Captain Kidd, being hanged for attacking the wrong ships. The Port Royal of our story was a safe harbor for pirates—until an earthquake destroyed it in 1692; divine retribution, according to some.

The pirates had a code of conduct called the Brotherhood that spelled out their rights, rules of behavior, and punishments; for example, fighting on board ship could result in both parties' being left to die on a deserted island.

Although the pirates' profession was harsh and dangerous, it was often better than their previous one. For many, their careers began as legitimate sailors, suffering under the lash of royal navies. After such a life, the freedom and camaraderie of piracy could be quite appealing.

DEATH IN THE
SERENE REPUBLIC

Venice, 1721

I T WAS THE EVE OF the Feast of the Ascension, a night filled with masked balls. Truth be told, in Venice one needed only a small excuse to hold a ball. And one needed even less excuse to wear a mask. Masks were almost as common a fashion accessory as gloves or hats.

There had even been a time, not long before, when women of society were forbidden to venture out in public without masks, an attempt by the Senate to discourage the wearing of showy jewelry. What would be the point of extravagant displays, the Senate reasoned, if no one could identify the wearer? The unexpected result of the law had been to allow high-class women to travel anonymously throughout the city, doing whatever pleased them.

Shortly after two on this early morning of revelry, Cesare Contini, heir to a long line of merchants, prepared to leave the Golden Ball. He stood on the portico of the Ca' d'Oro, the house of gold, facing the Grand Canal, and thanked his host, Count Franchetti, for the wonderful party.

"Your wife is not leaving with you?" asked the count, a bit confused.

"Too much wine gives me a headache," Cesare explained, massaging his temples. "And I don't wish to spoil Lucrezia's fun. Ah, here's Mario." The merchant stepped into a sumptuously painted gondola bearing his family crest. Half a league

away, at another palazzo along the Canal, Cesare's mistress had already left her ball of the evening and was walking purposefully to a point of rendezvous.

At about the same time, Lucrezia, Cesare's wife, was on the opposite side of the Ca' d'Oro. As her husband exited the party onto a canal, she was exiting onto a courtyard. Another guest, a man in a gold mask, rushed to stop her. Both revealed their faces and Lucrezia found herself staring up at Tomasso Romano.

"At the midnight dinner, when you let me touch your hand, you knew it was me."

"Yes," replied Lucrezia, trying to remain calm.

"I haven't seen you since your wedding." Repressed anger tinged the ex-suitor's voice. Lucrezia stepped back and, in her anxiety, twisted her papier-maché volto, accidentally breaking the silver mask in two.

"Here," Tomasso said. In a gallant gesture, he took her mask and replaced it with his own, identical except for the layer of gold paint.

She thanked her old sweetheart, donned the gold mask, and wrapped the hood of her crimson cape over her long, black curls. "We all make wrong choices in life, Tomasso. I am sorry."

Some passers-by later recalled seeing Lucrezia walking along Strada Nova. Or was it Riva delle Carbon? This was a night of parties and it was hard to recall. A handful of revelers did have a very clear memory of her pacing agitatedly by the Ponte Santa Marina, an elegant footbridge that spanned a spot where three canals joined. When the tide was flowing out to sea, as it was then, the currents could be treacherous.

It was nearly three in the morning, and the tired, drunken few looked on curiously as she walked to the middle of the bridge, removed her mask and hood, and, with a cry of despair, threw herself into the swirling black water.

In a city so accustomed to theatrics, it took several seconds for the terrible reality to sink in. The women stepped forward to the stone railing, scanning this rio, then that one, at the same time urging their men to do something, for heaven's sake. One man tried, doffing his cloak and diving into the cold darkness. But to no avail.

For two days, the body was not recovered. Doge Giovanni, chief magistrate of the Serene Republic, took a personal interest. Lucrezia had been born into one of Venice's richest families. Cesare's family wasn't far beneath hers, and if his fortune had dwindled…. Well, times change. None of the city's merchants were prospering as they had before the discovery of the New World.

Giorgio Presto was summoned for a private audience. The aide's usual function was to investigate the anonymous accusations of wrongdoing that citizens were free to place in the mouth of the stone box in the Doge's Palace. But on this day, the Doge had a different assignment for him.

"You must recover Lucrezia Contini's body," the city's ruler said. "This accident has devastated her family." The Doge emphasized the word *accident*. Suicides were barred from Christian burial. "Also, without a corpse, it will be harder for Signore Contini to settle his wife's estate. The body should have bloated and surfaced by now. See what you can do."

The aide went to work, sending men with nets to drag all the canals below the bridge of Santa Marina. Then he went to pay an official visit of condolence.

Ca' Contini was an old *fondaco*, a combination palazzo and warehouse left over from the 13th century, before the merchant kings had grown too grand to live above the store. Only a few of the *fondacos* remained, and their canal-level loading docks had been transformed into indoor boat slips for the family gondolas. As Giorgio rowed his *puppavino* up to the Contini mansion, he saw that the warehouse doors were closed.

Cesare Contini met him at the ornamental entrance and apologized for making him dock at the outside wharf. "Each year, we close off the indoor slips for a few days. Repair work. You can't imagine the rot in these ancient houses."

Giorgio explained his mission and Cesare thanked him for the Doge's sympathy. "Lucrezia should have come directly home. I went home myself and was worried when the hours passed and she didn't return."

Giorgio followed Cesare into the grand salon and was surprised to see two others there. The woman he recognized. Maria Garda was a young widow of questionable character. After her husband's death, a note had been slipped into the stone box, accusing Maria of his murder. Giorgio personally questioned her in a cell across the Bridge of Sighs from the Doge's Palace. Crossing the fateful bridge was by itself an ordeal. But Maria had withstood the hours of questioning with admirable will—or innocence. Maria had been Cesare's mistress even before his marriage to Lucrezia. Such things were common knowledge.

The salon's other occupant introduced himself. Tomasso Romano wore the plumed uniform of a palace guard. An ambitious, passionate man, Giorgio judged. "I'm glad the righteous magistrate has seen fit to investigate this tragedy," the guard said, throwing a scornful glance at Cesare. "Whatever happened on that terrible night, they drove her to it."

Giorgio realized that he had just walked in on a confrontation. He recalled vaguely now that Tomasso had once been an ardent suitor of the dead woman. Giorgio stood erect, tri-cornered hat in hand, and offered the condolences of the Doge and the Council of Ten.

Early the next morning, a vendor was maneuvering his *peata* through a little-used section of Rio del Pombo. He had made this same journey late the night before, his barge laden with fruits to sell at the campo markets. The vessel was considerably lighter now, but he was paying just as much attention to the shoals and banks. At least he thought so— until he hit something.

A golden shimmer sparkled from the shallow water. It

looked like a face. No, not a face. A mask. The handsome young vendor used an oar to try to pull the body to the surface. He saw the sash of a crimson cape tangled firmly around a submerged bar, holding the bloated corpse to its position, bobbing just below the surface.

An hour later, Giorgio was with the canal men as they dragged Lucrezia Contini from the water. The mask the vendor had seen was still clutched in the dead woman's hand.

"I have fulfilled the Doge's request," Giorgio thought. "The unfortunate woman can be buried. And yet..." He stared down at the body. "And yet something is wrong."

> *(1) Who, if anyone, was responsible for Lucrezia's death? (2) What were the circumstances behind her death? (3) What was the motive for the murder or suicide?*

If you've already solved this mystery, check the Solution on p. 133. To discover additional clues, turn to Gathering Evidence on p. 109.

HISTORICAL NOTES ON VENICE

TOWARD THE END of the Roman Empire, when the barbarians came down from the north, the people of eastern Italy sought refuge along the shallow sea, building a village on wooden posts pounded into the marshy seabed. The official date of founding this village, now called Venice, was 421.

This isolated fishing village evolved into a republic, with a senate and a chief magistrate (Doge) elected by the property-owning males. The citizens dubbed their city the Most Serene Republic. It remained a sleepy trading outpost until the time of the Christian crusades. Suddenly, the attention of Europe was focused east—to the Holy Lands and the rich trading routes to India and beyond. The Venetians had become expert sailors and no other city was in as strategic a location. In the space of a few decades, Venice grew into one of the richest cities in the world.

The city's slow decline began in the late 1400s. By then, the Turks had taken control over much of the eastern trading routes. And to the west, the riches of the Americas were being exploited by Spain, Portugal, France, and England, countries much better situated to take advantage of this New World.

For centuries, Venice remained a romantic party town, living off its past. It now exists almost entirely on tourism. The population is half what it was just fifty years ago. And the sheltering sea has added one more problem: too much water. Even a newly built series of dykes may not be enough to save Venice from sinking.

A CLOCKWORK MURDER

Switzerland, 1760

T HE BELLS OF THE VALANGIN town hall rang nine times, echoing through the sleepy streets. Hans, the watchman, had just finished closing the gates for the night. As the old man hobbled toward the square, he pulled out his pocket watch. It was his pride and joy, constructed within an iron musket ball and worth its weight in gold. Hans pried open the cover and shook his head. 9:05. There was no question in his mind that his watch was right and the town clock wrong.

Here in the Jura Valley, timekeeping was almost an art. The Swiss cantons prided themselves on the extravagance and accuracy of their clocks, even in small villages. Valangin had been as proud as any town, until a stroke of lightning from a spring storm fused several iron cogs together in their clock's delicate mechanism. The village commune had gathered in an emergency session and sent the mayor riding off to Bern in search of a master clockmaker. But the poor excuse of a clockmaker he returned with, this Carl Jurgen, curse his name....

Hans sighed and glanced up as darkness began to gather around the tower. A small stained-glass window just to the right of the clock face opened. An arm reached out the window, grabbed the minute hand and pulled it down. 9:06. Once a day at this time, that idiot Jurgen stopped his infernal fiddling and manually adjusted the hands, as if this would fool anyone.

Inside the tower, Carl Jurgen pulled his arm back through the window, latched it shut, then tried to wipe the fresh grease mark from his sleeve. "You cannot say I haven't oiled the workings, eh?" His attempt at humor did not impress his guest.

Mayor Birchenstock stood in the middle of the tower room, frowning. The young clockmaker had been here nearly a month, hammering and adjusting and rebuilding the intestines of his ailing patient, although he seemed to spend more time than necessary quenching his thirst at the Brown Bear Inn and romancing the innkeeper's daughter.

After three weeks, the clock had finally begun to work. Jurgen collected his gold and was halfway out of town before old Hans checked his pocket watch and realized that the huge clock was already losing time. A pair of farm boys dragged the reluctant clockmaker back and the mayor confiscated his fee. Now, a week later, the clock was still losing time. Perhaps it would never be fixed.

"It's not my fault," Jurgen said morosely. "You need a new weight mechanism."

"What?" Mayor Birchenstock could barely control his temper. This was a bold-faced lie, an excuse for the man's incompetence. If only he had listened to the commune and hired a well-known master instead of this charming young charlatan. Already tradesmen and travelers were spreading the word, laughing behind their hands at poor Valangin and its lazy clock. Right now the villagers blamed only Jurgen. How long before they started blaming him?

Without another word, the mayor turned his back, exited the clock room and stomped down the flights of wooden stairs. He had just rounded a corner near the bottom when he nearly collided with Marta Braun.

The innkeeper's daughter was carrying a tray of food in one hand and a tankard in the other. She spun around to avoid him, not spilling a crumb or a drop, then laughed with surprise. "Father doesn't like me to take him food," she said with a blush. "But Herr Jurgen works so hard. And his stories are so thrilling."

The mayor stood aside and let Marta continue up the stairs. When he reached the square, Mayor Birchenstock had a decision to make—turn left to home and hearth and the formidable Dame Birchenstock, or turn right to the Brown Bear Inn. He turned right.

Herman Braun took the mayor's personal stein down from its peg and filled it. The innkeeper seemed unusually quiet tonight, although when now and then he looked out the window toward the town hall, the mayor could guess what he was thinking.

The hall clock struck ten just as Marta walked through the heavy, beamed door with the empty tray. A flash in her eyes and a flutter of her hands seemed to confirm her father's worst fears. "You went to see that fool in the clock tower," he growled. Like the bear on his swinging sign, Herman Braun looked large and dangerous.

"So what if I did?" Marta answered with a defiance that sent chills down her father's spine. "Carl—Herr Jurgen—is the most exciting man I've ever met. The tales he tells of the world beyond this valley…"

"Enough," her father barked. "To speak of a stranger that way, and with your own marriage banns to be read in church this very Sunday. What would your fiancé think?"

"Johann knows how I feel about Carl. Maybe we should call off the wedding; maybe that's best." Marta left the words hanging as she crossed to stoke the fire, then refill the steins of Mayor Birchenstock and Hans the watchman, who had come in for a nightcap after his rounds.

The angry silence grew as the men drank and Marta washed down tables and her father polished the same keg spigot over and over. It was 10:10 by Hans's pocket watch when Johann Sensenig came through the door. The large, naturally cheerful man wished everyone a good evening, then went straight to Marta's side.

Her coolness toward the young herdsman was obvious. But Johann chose to ignore it, continuing to smile when no smiles were returned, reaching out to touch her hand on the table even as she drew it away.

Herman Braun saw all this and, growing too angry to stand still, disappeared into the kitchen. The mayor, just as uncomfortable, threw a few centimes on the oaken table, walked out to the lane, and turned toward home. Only Hans refused to play the diplomat and leave the couple alone. Slowly he drained his stein, then wiped his sleeve across his mouth.

"Come, escort me home," the old watchman said. Johann, always respectful of his elders, agreed with some reluctance. Before leaving, Johann wished his fiancée a good night's sleep.

The two men walked the narrow alleys of Valangin, discussing women and what they wanted and if they had changed at all in the forty years since Hans had been faced with similar problems. It was some time later when they circled around to the open, deserted square. By the light of the moon, Hans checked the time on the tower clock.

"Ten twenty-five? No!" Hans pulled out his own timepiece. "It's 10:31. The clock could not have lost so much." He peered into the dimness and saw the huge minute hand jerking back and forth between the same two painted lines. "Something is wrong."

Hans led the way to the town-hall tower, leaning on the younger man's arm as they climbed the four flights of stairs. A grinding, thumping sound, barely audible at ground level, grew louder and more ominous as they climbed.

At first glance, the clock room seemed empty of everything but the grinding and thumping. It was Johann who walked to the edge of the works and looked down. There was the young clockmaker, half a flight below them, wedged between the maws of the two largest gears.

Hans stepped forward and caught sight of the mangled body that had stopped the town clock at the fatal hour of 10:25. "God in heaven, he must have fallen."

Johann, with clearer, stronger eyes, saw the bloody gash on the rear of the dead man's head, far from any point of impact with the gears. Carl Jurgen had fallen, yes, but not by accident.

(1) Who killed Carl Jurgen? (2) What did the killer do to avoid detection? (3) What clue points to the killer?

If you've already solved this mystery, check the Solution on p. 134.
To discover additional clues, turn to Gathering Evidence on p. 110.

HISTORICAL NOTES ON SWISS CLOCKS & WATCHES

IN THE EARLY 1300s, the first public clocks began appearing on church towers in Central Europe, due mainly to the ingenious tinkering of Catholic monks. The trend spread across Europe, but the mechanics remained crude. The clocks would gain or lose several hours each day and were equipped with only one hand, the hour hand.

Over the next few centuries, the clocks' unreliable drive weights were replaced by pendulums, a concept first explored by Galileo. By 1721, the accuracy of pendulum clocks was improved to a gain or loss of just one second a day.

The Swiss became famous for timekeeping largely due to a single man, Abraham-Louis Breguet, recognized as the greatest watchmaker of all time.

Watches were first invented around 1500. Expensive and unreliable, they were initially the ornaments of royalty. Early models were worn around the neck or as broaches. Queen Elizabeth I owned a ring watch with an alarm that scratched her finger at the preset hour.

With the invention of the balance spring, watches became more reliable and less expensive, although at the time of our story, they were still not common possessions.

A SNAKE IN THE ASH PILE

California Gold Rush, 1851

MURDER WAS ALL TOO COMMON now, Doc Maynard thought, not for the first time. It didn't used to be that way. Two years ago, when the physician first arrived in the Sierra foothills, a miner could walk away from his stake and his kit and know that everything would be there when he got back.

But now, after traveling so long and putting up with so much privation, after getting here and finding so much of the gold already panned out, it was more than some men could take. About once a week, Doc would be digging a bullet from a whiskey-sodden corpse and glancing out his parlor window as a vigilante committee gathered in the street. They would search out the owner of the bullet, give him a quick trial and string him up before the light faded. On the map, their town was labeled Dry Diggings, but people were starting to call it Hangtown.

What made this murder different, thought Doc as he examined the scruffy, smelly body laid out on his own bed, was that it hadn't been committed in the heat of drunken passion. Someone had actually taken the time to kill Jesse Blackburn with poison. It seemed like more consideration than Jesse deserved.

It all began that morning. Abner Barnes, a Baptist preacher who'd abandoned his meager congregation for the lure of the gold fields, was just crossing Muddy Flats, half a mile out of town. He looked over to Jesse Blackburn's camp, ready to wave a greeting to the sour, unpleasant man and to the hired hands who slaved twelve hours a day at his sluice. But no one was there. Something was wrong. Even if Jesse were drunk in his cabin, Johnny Talaya or Hector Pleasant should have already been at work.

Abner glanced to the cabin, hoping to see Jesse's wife Mabel, one of the few bright spots in this stinky, muddy world. Instead he saw two men beside the timbered shack's only door. "Hello!" Abner shouted. A large, dark man was on his knees, bending over another man on the ground. "Johnny?" said Abner as he started to walk over. "What's wrong?"

Johnny was what they called a Kanaka, one of the native Hawaiians who'd come to San Francisco as sailors on the fast schooners that plied the Pacific. Like everyone else—farmers, preachers, dry goods merchants—most Kanakas had abandoned their ships or been abandoned by their bosses and made their way to the California hills. Many wound up as laborers, half a rung higher than the Blacks and Chinese, slaving on other men's long toms or risking their lives down other men's coyote holes.

The large, dark man spun around, a look of terror in his eyes. "He's been bit," Johnny said. The man moaning on the ground was Jesse Blackburn, incoherent from shock or pain or last night's whiskey; maybe all three.

"I saw the snake," Johnny said, pointing to the nearby brush. "Went into the bushes. Mr. Blackburn, he come running out of shack, holding leg and screeching fierce. We got sea snakes back home. Very big poison. Snakes here got poison, too. Yes?"

Abner asked Johnny what it looked like. From Johnny's description, it sounded like a rattlesnake. "You don't see many rattlers. Good gospel, Johnny, what you been doing?"

Jesse Blackburn's pant leg was torn open, exposing a

bloody ankle. The big Hawaiian was holding a knife in one hand. There was blood on the blade. "I suck out poison," Johnny said. "Is all right?" Abner had heard of this but had never seen it done. He was at a loss.

"Abner? Johnny? What happened?"

Mabel Blackburn was coming up the dirt path, pushing the empty wheelbarrow that had held this morning's meat pies. Mabel made a nice profit baking and selling pies to the womenless miners so unskilled in cooking. Behind her came Hector, the free Negro who sometimes walked with her as a bodyguard, not so much for Mabel's safety as for the money's. She could pocket two hundred dollars a day from her cooking, when Jesse wasn't around to drink and gamble it away.

Mabel saw her husband on the ground. "Jesse!" She seemed to know at once that it was more than just another case of his falling down drunk.

Johnny and Abner spouted out their stories. To Mabel's credit, she was quick to take control. A capable woman, Abner thought, adding it to her list of virtues.

"Hector, you stay and watch the camp. Johnny, come with me. Abner..." She couldn't order the minister around as she could her husband's workmen. "I'd appreciate it if you came along."

The men loaded Jesse in the back of the buckboard and set off for Hangtown and Doc Maynard's home. Doc placed the Indiana farmer-turned-miner in his own bed and for a while Jesse seemed to get better. One at a time, Doc allowed a visitor at the bedside—first Mabel, then Abner, his friend, and even Johnny, the hired man.

The case was touch and go, and Jesse's taste for the bottle seemed for once to be an advantage. "Nothing better for snake bite than whiskey," said Doc, repeating the old wives' tale. The words were barely out of his mouth when Jesse Blackburn's body convulsed and fought for breath and, a few seconds later, gave up the ghost.

Doc Maynard leaned over the lifeless figure, his eyes

focusing on the leg. "Something's wrong here," he said in his deep Southern drawl. Doc pointed to a small brown stain deep inside the cut-open wound. "Was this brown stuff here when you brought him in?"

"I don't remember," Mabel said with serious curiosity. "What does it mean?"

"Could mean poison," Doc said simply. "Give me some time with the body and maybe I'll know more."

Mabel and Abner and Johnny left the house in a daze. "Johnny?" said Mabel to the big Hawaiian. "Take the wagon and pick up supplies at Wang Fu's. He's got a list. Abner and I can walk."

As soon as Johnny left, Abner led the way back home. "Ain't too many rattlers in these parts," he said to Mabel. "If Jesse was drunk like he often is, it wouldn't take much to lay him out, cut open his leg and slip some poison into the wound. You call it a snakebite and no one will be the wiser."

Mabel's eyes grew wide. "No. Johnny cut the leg in order to suck out the poison, not to...What reason would he have...?" She stopped. Of course Johnny had a reason to kill. No one treated hired help worse than Jesse. For the past two months, he'd held back their pay, always giving some excuse or other. Neither Johnny nor Hector had taken it well.

Black Hector had been saving money to buy his family's freedom back in east Texas. Just yesterday he'd threatened to stab Jesse if he didn't pay their wages. Jesse made all sorts of excuses and both men had no choice but to believe him.

"Johnny knows *I'll* pay them," Mabel whispered. "Out of my own pocket if need be."

"I'm gonna check around Johnny's tent," said Abner. He saw Hector in the distance and waved to him to wait up.

"OK," said Mabel in a weak voice. "I want some time alone." Then she cut across Muddy Flats and disappeared into a grove of aspens.

Johnny's and Hector's tents stood side by side in a ravine not far from the Blackburn cabin. As they walked, Abner explained his suspicions to Hector. At first the freed slave didn't want to have anything to do with looking for his boss's killer. But Hector wasn't the type to argue much. The two men searched Johnny's tent, found nothing, then walked out of the ravine and toward the cabin.

Meanwhile in Hangtown, Doc Maynard finished his examination. From the minute he'd mentioned poison, he knew Johnny would be a suspect. Could Hawaiian Johnny really be a killer? He doubted it.

"If I can stop one unearned lynching in these parts..." Doc left the thought unfinished as he threw on his coat and headed out the door. "All I need is some evidence."

(1) Who killed Jesse Blackburn? (2) How was he killed? (3) What evidence points to the killer?

If you've already solved this mystery, check the Solution on p. 135. To discover additional clues, turn to Gathering Evidence on p. 111.

HISTORICAL NOTES ON GOLD RUSH FEVER

IN JANUARY OF 1848, James Marshall was constructing a sawmill along the American River when he discovered a golden nugget in the riverbed. He looked and saw another nugget, then another. Neither Marshall nor his employer, John Sutter, was happy about this. They were building what they hoped would be an agricultural empire and the last thing they wanted was an invasion of gold seekers overrunning their land. They agreed to keep the discovery secret, and their plan worked—for a while.

Rumors began circulating, but no one quite believed them, until Sam Brannan, a store owner and newspaperman, heard the news. Brannan immediately bought up every shovel and pickaxe he could lay his hands on and then ran through the streets of San Francisco, shouting that gold had been found. People finally paid attention, and mining pans that he had bought for twenty cents were now selling for fifteen dollars. Sam Brannan, who never mined for gold, quickly became California's richest man.

By 1849, men were flocking to northern California from all over the world. It took four months of arduous travel to reach the gold fields, either across the barren plains and mountains or by ship around the tip of South America. Tens of thousands came, believing the wildest of stories. An ad in an Indiana paper promoted a secret lotion. All you had to do was rub it on your body and roll down a hill. The lotion would make gold stick to you and, by the time you reached the bottom, you would be set for life. One lotion supposedly worked for gold. Another worked for silver.

What set the California gold rush apart from earlier strikes is that the discovery occurred in an unsettled, largely owner-less territory. There were few laws and even fewer families to act as social restraints to the wild young fortune seekers.

As for John Sutter and his dream of an agricultural empire.... Although in a perfect position to prosper from the early days of the rush, Sutter never caught gold fever. The '49ers, as they were dubbed, stole his crops, trampled his farms, and tore down his fort for building material. John Sutter, on whose land the gold was found, died a bankrupt man.

FIRE & RAIN

Great Chicago Fire, 1871

*J*UDGE ELMER CRAMDON ENTERED HIS house soaked to the skin and smelling of wet smoke. The entire city smelled of wet smoke. The day's downpour had succeeded in doing what days of firefighting hadn't, putting out the last embers of the conflagration that had devastated the heart of Chicago and left a third of its 300,000 citizens homeless.

"Where's your new umbrella?" Vera Cramdon asked as she unbuttoned her husband's sopping coat and hung it in the closet. The judge looked slightly shocked to discover his loss.

"You're so forgetful," Vera chided. "How is everything with the Common Council? How is Mayor Mason?"

Elmer had spent much of the morning discussing the provisions for martial law and the return of essential services. "Sheridan, the war hero, has taken charge," he informed his wife. "Unfortunately, the fire came at the worst time for city officials. Joseph Medill plans to oppose us in the elections. Stricter building codes! Baa! It doesn't take a genius to suggest stricter codes now. But Medill's *Tribune* will take up the cause and his reporters will fan the flames." He winced at his unfortunate choice of metaphor.

"The city was growing so fast," Vera said consolingly. "Even if you had strict codes, people wouldn't have obeyed, especially in the poor districts where this whole catastrophe began."

"At least the *Tribune*'s new fireproof building went up in smoke," Elmer laughed as he glanced out a side window. "Speaking of the *Tribune,* there's someone over at Rory Johnson's house. They're arguing."

"Let me see." In a second, Vera joined him. Just half a week earlier it would have been impossible to see from the judge's parlor window to the *Tribune* editor's. There would have been a stable and another house in the way. But the fire in its quixotic path had left, here and there, a few buildings completely untouched. On this block, three homes stood erect and whole amid the ashy rubble: the judge's, the editor's, and ironically enough, one belonging to the president of a fire insurance company.

"Too late," Elmer said, as Vera looked out the window. "They moved away. I couldn't see who; except it was a man and he looked angry."

"The whole city has a right to be angry at Mr. Rory Johnson," Vera said. "His paper will vilify every decent official in town, mark my words. He'll use this fire to accuse everyone of graft and profiteering and criminal neglect. By the way," she added, having reminded herself of criminal neglect, "is it true what they say about that Irish woman?"

Judge Cramdon nodded. "Mrs. Kate O'Leary. It started in her barn, although her own house not ten feet away somehow escaped the flames. Some say it was her cow kicking over a lamp. Some say it was her boys sneaking a smoke. There are some who even think..." He stopped.

"It was the French radicals," Vera Cramdon said, completing his sentence. "With their crazy ideas of the Paris commune. I knew it! They set their own city on fire and now they send someone to Chicago to do the same."

"Perhaps," said the judge, tiring of his wife's bilious theories. "I'm going into my study." And the judge sauntered into the next room, closing the door behind him.

Judge Cramdon hadn't been in his study for more than five minutes when a gunshot echoed across the North Division neighborhood. When Vera opened the study door, she found him staring out the window. "A gunshot," she gasped.

"Two of 'em," the judge corrected her. "From Rory Johnson's house." Without another word, the middle-aged jurist went into the parlor, retrieved his wet coat from the closet and strode into the street. Mrs. Cramdon grabbed her own coat and followed.

The rain had stopped, but the rubble-strewn block was still deserted, all except for an artist who had set up an easel in the middle of the street. Cramdon had seen these entrepreneurs of disaster already popping up across the city, artists sketching the dramatic ruins, hoping to sell their works to the illustrated papers or to tourists. "Window. Over there," the man called out as he left his easel and crossed to the Cramdons. He spoke with a French accent and was pointing toward the Johnson home. Even from here, they could see the shattered side window.

"I was looking there when it happened. Bang! Right through the window."

"Did you see anyone?" the judge asked the rumpled young man.

"No," the man said almost apologetically. "Must've been shot from inside."

The judge was about to ask if the Frenchman had seen anyone leaving but then realized the front door wasn't visible from here. A minute later, the three arrived at the door and were met by a fourth. Walter Root, insurance company president, the only other homeowner left on the block, met them on the front steps. "I was just returning," said the heavy-set businessman, motioning toward a trap and horse tied to a blackened stone post by his own townhouse. "I heard a gunshot."

They tried the thick oak door and found it locked. It took an iron bar scavenged from the street and the strength of all three men to break it open. Rory Johnson was a bachelor and, like everyone else, had given his servants time off to deal with their own losses. "Mr. Johnson?" Judge Cramdon called out. When there was no response, he led the way back to the side library.

From the library doorway, they saw the crumpled body. There was no gun in sight, just a bloody candlestick and several deep gashes on Rory Johnson's head. "Keep Mrs. Cramdon out," the judge instructed the two men, then walked gingerly into the room and knelt down. "Here's the gun," he said and reached across to the far side of the corpse.

Walter Root joined the judge. The gun was a Colt 0.36, the type made popular by the Texas Rangers. "I didn't know Rory was left-handed."

"Did you know him well?" asked Cramdon.

"We met a few times," Root admitted. "He carried a gun everywhere. Dozens of men wanted him dead, so he said, for all the dark secrets he knew. He was at my house this afternoon."

"Why?" asked Mrs. Cramdon. She had recovered from the shock and now entered the room. "You weren't one of the dozens, I trust."

Root's laugh was hollow. "My insurance firm, as the world will soon discover, is going bankrupt. We can't possibly settle all the claims. A fire of this magnitude...Rory accused me of hiding funds, of declaring a false bankruptcy. Rory and his damned publisher want to unearth some scandal from this tragedy. Crooked business dealings, crooked officials, some international plot. Rory was looking everywhere."

The room fell silent for a moment as each mulled over Root's words. "What in the world happened?" Vera Cramdon finally asked.

"Well," her husband volunteered as he crossed to the broken window. "I saw Mr. Johnson at this very spot arguing with someone. About five minutes later I heard the shots."

"I didn't see a soul come or leave," said the French artist. "Of course, I had no view of the front door."

"It seems like Rory used the gun to try to protect himself," Root hypothesized. "The shot missed and went through the window glass."

"Might the killer still be here?" asked Vera. Then she turned and caught a glimpse out the broken front door. "Oh, dear. If someone was inside, we gave him an escape. He's long gone by now."

The men all agreed, but half-heartedly. Instinctively they knew that Rory Johnson's killer was still in the house.

(1) Who killed Rory Johnson? (2) What was the sequence of events? (3) What piece of evidence points to the killer?

If you've already solved this mystery, check the Solution on p. 136.
To discover additional clues, turn to Gathering Evidence on p. 112.

HISTORICAL NOTES ON THE GREAT CHICAGO FIRE

FOR THOUSANDS OF years, fire was the most feared enemy of any city. Before the advent of fire-resistant materials and modern firefighting techniques, fires would often destroy entire metropolises, from ancient Rome to Restoration London.

The summer and fall of 1871 had been a particularly dry period in the mostly wooden city of Chicago. Then on Sunday, October 8, just after 9 P.M., flames broke out in the barn of the Patrick O'Leary family. Legend has it that Mrs. O'Leary's cow kicked over a lantern—and that explanation remains a possibility. Firefighters responded, but were exhausted from having fought a large fire just the previous day. Destruction spread for two days, until heavy rains on October 10 helped douse the flames. Over 300 people died and the heart of the city was destroyed.

The city rebuilt quickly. Just 22 years later, Chicago hosted the Columbian Exposition, celebrating the 400th anniversary of Columbus's arrival in America. The site for this world's fair had been hotly contested among the largest U.S. cities. The long competition delayed the exposition for a year (until 1893) and led one New York editor to decry the Chicago delegation's vocal boosterism. He labeled Chicago "that windy city." And the nickname stuck.

THE RIPPER'S LAST VICTIM

London, 1888

T HEY THINK HE STRANGLES 'EM dead before he cuts 'em up. That's what they're saying." Ruthie Tanner shivered, then ordered another pint.

For months now people had been talking of little else, especially in London's East End, most especially in this pub, the Ten Bells, where two of Jack the Ripper's women had been seen shortly before their grisly deaths. The latest victim, Mary Kelly, had been a regular at the Ten Bells, dropping in to drink and sometimes to pick up a bit of company for the evening.

Danny Wainwright nodded. "My Jilly says he's got big hands; she recalls it clear."

"Your Jilly?" Amos growled as he delivered Ruthie's pint. It hadn't been so long ago that Jilly was Amos's girl. After an evening of pouring drinks, he'd been proud to step out with the pretty little singer, even if she wasn't as young as she'd once been. And now, to see her married to a fast-talking character like Wainwright—it was almost more than Amos could bear.

"She really saw him then?" asked Ruthie, her voice tinged with jealousy. Jilly Jones, in one of those fateful accidents of life, had exchanged a few words with the Ripper on the last night of September, just seconds before Catharine Eddowes's body was found in Mitre Square.

Jilly became an instant celebrity. Her popularity at Farrow's Music Hall soared. She had even taken to finishing her performance by describing the Ripper, re-enacting their conversation, then issuing a defiant boast that she could identify the villain on sight and would gladly send Jacky to the gallows.

Ruthie's own engagement at Farrow's had been cancelled to make room for Jilly's expanded act. But that would soon change, she told herself. Ruthie was younger and prettier— and she could even sing. Already the thirstiest members of the audience were starting to retrieve drinks from the bar during Jilly's dramatic re-enactment.

"'Course she saw him," Danny replied. "Jilly and me was out pub crawling that night when she steps into an alley to relieve herself. Couple minutes later, she comes out, all ashy faced. A strange, dangerous man had talked to her in there. Then we hears the police whistle."

When the young reporter from the *East London Observer* entered the Ten Bells, Danny jumped up to greet him. "Thanks for coming so late. Jilly's show just finished. She'll be here any minute."

"Does she really remember new clues about the Ripper?" the reporter asked suspiciously, taking out his notepad and pencil. "It's been weeks since she saw him."

"She always remembered," Danny said smoothly. "She's just been too scared to tell every detail. But after this last bit of slaughter, my brave lass will risk all—as long as you print her complete words with a nice pen and ink portrait on your front page."

Ruthie let out a little moan of despair. It's going to start up all over again, she thought. Amos Pickering glowered from behind the bar. Jilly's opportunistic husband was going to squeeze every farthing he could out of this situation, thought he. And the dark, mustachioed man who'd been sitting by himself in the corner silently got up and headed for the pub's rear door. No one had any idea what might be on his mind.

The clock on the wall struck midnight as Danny bought the reporter a pint of bitter. "I gotta go watch me brother's brats," Ruthie said. She plopped down a shilling and headed for the door. Ruthie's brother was a fish porter at the docks. His shift started at midnight, although Ruthie usually didn't show up at his flat until after one. Tonight, she'd get there early.

"It's dead tonight. I'm closing up." Amos rushed the two men through their ales, then ushered them out into an alley. "Think I'll meander up to the Horn of Plenty," he yawned, then turned the corner onto the main thoroughfare of Commercial Road.

Danny fumbled nervously for his pocket watch. "I don't know what's keeping Jilly. What say we head over to the music hall? We'll probably meet her on the way."

Night fog drifted in from the Thames, diffusing the gassy glow from the street lamps. As they walked, going from populated streets to winding lanes, Danny kept up a monologue, promoting his bride's talent and integrity, even her financial acumen. "No singer in Whitechapel has done better." The further they wandered into the shadowy alleys, the louder he seemed to speak. "S'got her own house, she does, free and clear, plus something in the bank."

The reporter was the first to hear it, the sound of scuffling and a woman's muffled cry. With a raised hand, he halted Danny in mid-sentence.

"Help! Someone help me!" The words echoed in the fog, sounding desperate and strangled.

"Jilly?" Danny turned in circles, trying to pinpoint the source. "Where are you, Jilly?" There were no more words, only the sound of footsteps.

Danny listened until the footsteps stopped. "Over here," he said and led the way through an archway into the narrow alley known as George Yard.

Jilly Jones lay motionless on the ground, face up, the crown of her head facing them as they approached. "Get a copper,"

Danny yelled as he knelt by the body. "Quick. On the run."

The reporter rushed out onto Wentworth Street and, as luck would have it, within seconds found a constable making his rounds. When they returned to the site, Danny hadn't moved. He was kneeling behind her head and sobbing her name. "Jilly, my lass. The brute has strangled her dead."

Inspector Abberline gazed down at the body lying on the morgue slab. "Looks like he didn't have time to cut her, but she's just as dead."

"Not all murdered women between Spitalfields and Whitechapel are the Ripper's victims," Sergeant Godley reminded his superior.

That was true. Of the seven, now eight, women the newspapers were listing as victims, only five were confirmed as being killed by the beast who had labeled himself Jack in those sickening, taunting notes.

"We're checking out the patrons of Farrow's Music Hall," added Godley. "Perhaps one of them followed her."

"Good," said Abberline approvingly. "Let's also check out the people at Ten Bells. According to that reporter, they all heard Danny Wainwright say that she was coming to the pub from Farrow's. George Yard is on a direct route between the two."

"Already done," Godley said and opened his notebook. "Ruthie Tanner claims she went straight from the pub to her brother's place in Pinchin Street. The little nipper who unlatched the door for her, he says the Bow Bells struck midnight just a few minutes before she came."

"Hmm. A nephew might just lie. What about the barman?"

"Amos Pickering says he was drinking at the Horn of Plenty. No one remembers him specifically."

"Seems odd to close down your own pub, then go off drinking at another. Any luck tracking down this stranger with the mustaches?"

Godley flipped a page. "Name's Ezekiel Braun. A genteel, shabby foreigner, like a few of the Jack witnesses describe.

Pretends not to speak much English. But I did get him to swear that he went from the Ten Bells to St. Botolph's in Aldgate High Street to light a candle and say a prayer."

"St. Botolph's?" the inspector muttered. "Isn't that called the Prostitute's Church?"

"Right. It's also the spot where Catharine Eddowes was seen the night of her murder. Shall I bring him in for questioning?"

"Let's examine a few pieces of evidence first. Then we'll know who to bring in."

(1) Who killed Jilly Jones? (2) How did the killer establish an alibi? (3) What was the motive?

If you've already solved this mystery, check the Solution on p. 137.
To discover additional clues, turn to Gathering Evidence on p. 113.

HISTORICAL NOTES: WHAT HAPPENED TO JACK?

JACK THE RIPPER was not the first serial killer in history, just the first famous one. He happened to appear in one of the world's largest cities at a time when literacy was high and newspapers had become a major force in daily life. Between August and mid-November of 1888, London was transfixed daily by the latest rumors, copycat murders, and hoaxes which only served to mythologize a bloody killer, and muddy the investigation.

The number of Ripper victims is a matter of dispute. One well-known historian concluded that there were at least four, probably six. The newspapers of the day raised the total to eleven. Murders of women were not unusual in London's East End, and the press was eager to attribute any brutal attack to the "beast from hell." All of the Ripper victims were prostitutes, making them easy targets, and all were thought to be drunk at the time of their deaths.

The killer's original nickname in the press was Leather

Apron, a reference to a leather apron found beside the second confirmed victim. But on September 25, the Central News Agency received a letter bragging about the crimes and signed, "Yours truly, Jack the Ripper." This letter, along with others received by the police, is now thought to be a hoax. A package, received in mid-October, contained half a human kidney, supposedly taken from Catharine Eddowes. But this, too, may have been a hoax. Medical students of the period were not above such gruesome pranks.

Speculation on the identity of the Ripper has not slowed in the hundred-plus years since. Over two dozen suspects have been suggested, including the professor and children's book author Lewis Carroll and a woman nicknamed Jill the Ripper. The most popular suspect, accused in multiple books and movies, is Prince Albert Victor, grandson of Queen Victoria. The royal family supposedly knew of the murders and engaged in an elaborate cover-up. Prince Eddy, second in line to the throne, died of influenza in 1892.

The most recent solution was proposed by mystery author Patricia Cornwell. Her candidate is Walter Sickert, a famous artist of the period. Her theory is supported by partial DNA evidence lifted from some of the Ripper letters. But most, if not all, of the letters are now thought to be hoaxes. So, the question is still open. Was Sickert the Ripper? Or was he a prankster?

We'll leave the final theory to Frederick Abberline, the real-life model for our own inspector. His prime suspect was Severin Klosowski, a Polish immigrant. Klosowski, a barber experienced with blades, was suspected years later in a similar prostitute murder in the United States and, back in London, was eventually convicted of poisoning his three wives. When Sergeant Godley, the model for our own Sergeant Godley, arrested Klosowski, the retired Inspector Abberline congratulated him. "You've got Jack the Ripper at last!"

We'll probably never know for sure.

THE ECCENTRIC
ALCHEMIST

Prague, 1894

COUNT MIROSLAV TYRS ADJUSTED THE clips on the voltaic cell and continued his demonstration. Lumps of iron ore and coke were spinning slowing in a revolving kiln. Through an isinglass window they could see the rocks absorb the electricity and begin to heat up.

"My passion has always been alchemy," the count admitted shyly.

Herbert Greenway laughed. "You mean like turning lead into gold?" the American millionaire said in passable German. "Is that what this is about? That's a fairy tale."

Karel, the count's nephew, bristled. "Isaac Newton did experiments in alchemy. It has an ancient tradition, especially here. Emperor Rudolf even set up a company of alchemists in the far corners of Prague Castle."

"This is not alchemy." The count stared daggers at his nephew. He needed the American's goodwill, needed his money, in order to finance his new iron-making scheme. "But it was while working with lead and gold that I happened upon this process. No more need for pig iron and a Bessemer furnace. Combine electricity with the right elements and voltage, and you get a harder, purer iron than previously possible."

Rolf Berger observed the three men and didn't know what to think. As the emperor's emissary, Rolf was wary of Count

Tyrs. The eccentric aristocrat was descended from one of the noblest of Czech families. But what riches hadn't been lost in the religious wars had been squandered by the count himself in his endless experiments. Just the year before, he had persuaded investors to back him in a search for a universal solvent, only to call off his quest when he couldn't find any container that could hold it without disintegrating.

Rolf, an old school chum of Karel's, had always liked Count Tyrs. But he could never decide if the alchemist was a swindler or a true believer. Today Rolf was here as a curious friend. Tomorrow might be different.

The four men retreated from the heat. The count checked his temperature gauge, then flipped an electrical switch at just the right moment, stopping the revolving kiln. Using a steel bar, Count Tyrs opened a latch and poured the molten iron into a mold.

The American inspected the cooling iron and was impressed. "Andrew Carnegie would give his eyeteeth to see this," he said in an awed whisper. "Count Tyrs, I think you and I can do business."

The count puffed out his chest with pleasure. "Wonderful."

Rolf stayed for supper and afterwards wandered into the display hall. Through the centuries, the Tyrs family had amassed an unparalleled collection of gold figurines, some dating back to the earliest days of the Holy Roman Empire. The small, jewel-decorated statuettes represented a high point of Czech workmanship—treasures, but ones that the Tyrses couldn't easily profit from. Emperor Franz Joseph himself had forbidden them from splitting up the collection or allowing it to be sold outside the Hapsburg domain.

Rolf circled the room, admiring the artifacts in their simple, glass-fronted cupboards. "Are you ready to head back to the Stare Mesto?"

Rolf looked up to see Karel Tyrs standing in the doorway already dressed in his riding cloak. "Yes, of course."

The two friends bade farewell to Count Tyrs and the

American, then mounted Karel's open carriage and began the brisk ride from the estate back to the old section of Prague.

"Is Herr Greenway staying with your uncle?" Rolf asked.

"Yes," answered Karel. The young man seemed in a foul mood. "They met yesterday in Vienna. He was coming to Prague and offered Uncle a seat in his private railway car. You know Uncle Miroslav. He becomes fast friends with anyone who has money."

"You disapprove?"

Karel shrugged. "So many of Uncle's projects fail, or they cost more to operate than they bring in. Every investor in the Austro-Hungarian Empire has lost money. But what if this iron-making process actually works? It would leave Bohemia and make more millions for America, millions that belong here. It's not right."

Rolf understood. Karel was one of the new breed of nationalists, young men determined to preserve the Czech ways, working behind the scenes, never quite breaking the law, hoping for independence from the Hapsburg throne.

"Don't forget who I am," Rolf warned his friend. "You must be careful."

Two days later, Rolf received an urgent message and rode out to the Tyrs estate. The count was waiting for him, looking frantic. "Herr Greenway has vanished," he whispered. "Yesterday, my man Vaclav drove him into Prague to tour the city. The American wanted to walk across Charles Bridge to view the statues and the scenery. Vaclav drove the carriage across and waited on the other side. But he never came. The man disappeared."

"What do you think happened?"

"A rich American in a city full of cutthroat gypsies?" Count Tyrs shuddered at the thought. "I'd inform the police, but they won't do anything. What scandal! He was my guest."

"And a potential investor," Rolf observed.

Rolf agreed to conduct an unofficial search. Greenway, he

discovered, had not registered with the American consul, nor was he known by any of the foreign contingent at the Grand Hotel. Hospitals and morgues had no body matching the description. It was as if the foreigner had fallen off the face of the earth—or been pushed.

After a day and a half of fruitless searching, Rolf returned to his lodgings. His doorman raced up with a telegram. Count Tyrs, it seemed, had found something. An hour later, Rolf Berger was in a guest bedroom of the manor house inspecting a man's scarf and a shabby box of matches. "Hotel Club," he read from the box top. "Prague."

"Herr Greenway never stayed at a hotel," the count explained. "He was my guest from his arrival, or so I believed. Today we found these in his room, fallen behind a dresser. I wired you right away. What could it mean?"

Rolf pocketed the matchbox. "I don't know."

Before leaving, the imperial emissary interviewed the coachman. Vaclav was a swarthy, angry-looking man who might have possessed a little gypsy blood. "It was as the count told you," he assured Rolf. "The American wanted to see the sights. I drove him straight to Charles Bridge, where he got out of the carriage. He was carrying a business valise; nothing else."

Before heading back to Prague, Rolf stopped at the local village. An old peasant friend still owned a pair of blood-hounds. Rolf gave the peasant the scarf and instructions. "Have them smell out this scent around the Tyrs estate. And don't let Vaclav or anyone else know what you're up to."

It was late that night when Rolf arrived in the dark crooked alleys of Prague's lesser town. The Hotel Club was an old stagecoach inn that had deteriorated into a maze of cheap rented rooms. It was hardly the place one would expect to house an American millionaire. With some difficulty, Rolf tracked down the porter and described his quarry.

"A tall man who speaks bad German?" the man said eagerly as he eyed Rolf's uniform. Everyone connected with the court of Vienna had some sort of uniform and often they came in handy. "Yes. Room 305. Let me present you, dear sir."

The porter grabbed a set of keys from a letter box and led the way. When no one responded to his knocks and repeated entreaties, he used a key.

The door to 305 swung open to reveal a room just as shabby as the hallway; shabbier, if you counted the body sprawled out on the floor. Rolf recognized the man—Herbert Greenway, surrounded by a pool of blood, a dagger handle ornamenting his chest. The body was already cold and beginning to smell.

(1) Who killed Herbert Greenway? (2) What was the motive? (3) What evidence led Rolf to the right suspect?

If you've already solved this mystery, check the Solution on p. 137.
To discover additional clues, turn to Gathering Evidence on p. 114.

HISTORICAL NOTES ON ALCHEMY

AS PEOPLE STRUGGLED between the worlds of superstition and science, alchemy often took hold of the popular imagination. One legendary ingredient was the philosophers' stone, an elusive powder that, combined with a magical incantation, was supposed to turn lead into gold. The roots of alchemy can be traced from ancient Egypt through Greece to the Arab world. It emerged again in Medieval Europe. In the 16th century, Emperor Rudolf made a concerted effort, setting up alchemy labs in his castle and convincing much of the Prague nobility to experiment on their own.

To the medieval mind, the concept was logical. After all, iron could be transformed into steel, sand could become glass, and with a recipe stolen from the Far East, clay could be made into fine porcelain. But alchemy could also be a dangerous pursuit. In times of religious fervor, alchemists were executed for witchcraft, hanged from gilded gallows.

CURSE OF THE PHARAOH

Egypt, 1923

EATH SHALL COME ON SWIFT Wings to Him Who Disturbs the Peace of the King."

These ominous words, a curse from beyond the grave, were reportedly etched over the doorway of King Tutankhamen's tomb. They weren't.

Like so many of the so-called facts, this curse was invented by newspaper reporters who weren't about to let the truth stand between them and a good story. If there had been such a curse, I should have been the first one struck down. For it was I, Howard Carter of Norfolk, England, who was most responsible for discovering the tomb and removing its riches.

The legend of the curse dogged us almost from the very start. On November 4, 1922, after many years of false hopes, my workman uncovered sixteen steps leading down into the sand of the Valley of the Kings. For the first time, we knew that a tomb of high rank awaited us.

That evening I returned to my house in Luxor to find my Egyptian manservant in a state of nervous agitation. A cobra, it seemed, had killed a pet canary I had brought over with me from England.

"The pharaoh's serpent ate the bird," he said in a breathless moan. The cobra was, of course, one of the pharaoh's symbols. "This is a warning. You must not disturb the tomb."

My response was a practical one, telling him to make sure the cobra was no longer in the house.

Three weeks later, with my financial patron, Lord Carnarvon, by my side, I broke a hole into the outer burial chamber and caught my first glimpse of the treasure that would make "King Tut" a household name.

Shortly thereafter, Lord Carnarvon died from a mysterious fever. On that same night, in faraway England, Carnarvon's favorite hunting dog also died, and the world was suddenly convinced of the pharaoh's curse. Since then, they have connected over twenty other deaths to the curse, from Arthur Mace, an American archeologist who assisted me, to my own dear wife.

Time has passed. The year is now 1938. I'm a man in my mid-sixties. And I suppose whenever I die, of whatever cause, it will be attributed to this same vengeful curse.

If you believe in such nonsense, there is little I can say to dissuade you. But I can tell you of one death that was in no way caused by a curse—for it was a deliberate, cold-blooded murder. I am free to tell the story now, since the players in this drama have all preceded me to the grave.

After the first whirlwind of fame, the flood of official visits to the tomb dwindled. But our work continued. My team was increasingly engaged in the laborious process of cataloging hundreds of delicate artifacts under the hot Egyptian sun.

Abdel Effendi, from Egypt's Department of Antiquities, had joined our desert camp. The small, serious scholar was charged with safeguarding his nation's heritage, and he trusted no one. Throughout each long day, Effendi would list off the statues and jewelry and funerary items emerging from the chambers. After sunset, he would still be at work, checking rumors among the local workmen and sticking his generous nose into every cubbyhole where a thief might hide a priceless artifact.

The routine went unbroken until the last Saturday in May, 1923. I was about to leave camp and join my dear wife in Luxor when the sound of crashing rocks caught my ear and stopped my heart. Fearing a collapse, I raced out of my tent.

"Is it the tomb?" I cried to everyone and no one.

Dr. Jules Grissard stood in front of his own tent. "No," he assured me. "It came from over there." He led the way across camp toward the abandoned, empty tunnels we had dug during the nine previous, fruitless years of our search.

At first, all seemed fine. One of the tunnels had fallen harmlessly into itself. And then we saw the robe and the human hand. Immediately, the workmen began digging. "It's Effendi," said Dr. Grissard. "Mohammed, the kit." He gave the foreman a key from his watch fob and pointed him toward the medical tent.

As the Egyptian foreman lumbered off, we saw that a lucky placement of fallen boulders had prevented Abdel Effendi from being crushed and killed outright. "I must speak," he said weakly. "Important."

"Save your strength," the French physician admonished.

Mohammed returned with a medical kit. "Brand new," he said proudly as he returned the key to the doctor. Inside the kit were perfect rows of white bottles and wrapped gauze.

Grissard grabbed the bottle of smelling salts and turned back to his patient. We all stepped aside, giving him room. But it was no use. Less than a minute later, the Egyptian official gave out a last little gasp.

"He's dead," Grissard said and absently placed the bottle of salts in his pocket.

"The pharaoh's curse," Mohammed muttered darkly.

I didn't scold him for his irresponsible words, said within earshot of so many. Perhaps I should have.

Within an hour, we were on our way to Luxor with Effendi's body, leaving a regiment of soldiers to guard the excavation site in our absence. At the banks of the Nile, we dismounted our horses to rest while the servants loaded the ferry.

We were all of us quite upset by the accident, especially, it seemed, Mustaf, an Egyptian student from the University of Cairo. The boy was small and slight, with a usually sunny smile. Mustaf was not smiling now. He and Dr. Grissard sat under a stand of palms, munching from a bowl of figs that Mohammed, the foreman, had set out.

"The rocks should not have fallen," Mustaf said. "I was in charge of old tunnels. They were all secure, I swear." And here he lowered his voice. "Did Effendi say anything? Before he died, he spoke of something important…"

"Yes, he did," Grissard said with a scowl. "But that's between him and me—and the authorities." Grissard refused to elaborate, but took another fig and slipped it into his mouth.

The ferry had returned for another loading. Dr. Grissard untied his horse and pushed his way to the head of the queue. But the horse was tramping too close to the bulrushes. Several of us saw the cobra slither from its nest and coil itself to attack. We shouted a general warning, but too late.

In the flash of an eye it was over. The horse bolted wildly. Dr. Grissard tried to control the reins, but he was dragged under the pounding hooves, his ribs crushed by the panicking beast.

Grissard was still conscious when Mustaf knelt down by his side. The doctor seemed desperate to speak, his mouth an inch from the student's ear. And then, before he could say a word, his eyes rolled back and his body went limp. "Mere fainted," Mustaf said, allaying the worst of our fears. Grissard's chest pulsed in quick, shallow breaths. "Quick, the salts."

"In his pocket," Mohammed said.

I reached into Grissard's jacket and retrieved the small brown bottle of salts. Mustaf, flustered and anxious, grabbed it. He was just placing it under the physician's nose, when the injured man opened his eyes.

Grissard seemed confused and disoriented. And then, as if he were recalling some unspeakable horror, his eyes widened. "Murder," he gasped. Twice more he gasped. When he went limp this time, there was no reassuring pulsing of his chest.

"Did he say murder?" asked I. Those at my side assured me that this had indeed been the French doctor's last word.

I was stunned. In just one day, the Valley of the Kings had taken the lives of two of my closest associates.

The Egyptian laborers began milling about the ferry landing, jabbering in hushed tones. I myself would have almost been persuaded to believe in their demonic curse, had it not been for the doctor's one dying word, "Murder."

"How could it be murder?" I asked myself, stumbling away from the doctor's mangled body. The cobra had been real; I'd seen it myself. The horse panicked, as any horse would. How could a murderer have arranged that?

Mohammed slowly returned the men to their tasks. The stolid, competent man personally took charge of the water bottles and foodstuffs, restoring everything to the camel pouches in preparation for our river crossing. I was only marginally aware of his actions, until he tapped me on the shoulder and showed me the still unpacked bowl of figs.

"Smell," Mohammed whispered, holding the bowl up to my nose.

I didn't have to breathe deeply. The smell was pungent and unmistakable. "Ammonia," I whispered back. And underneath the ammonia was another smell, something bitter that I couldn't quite place.

"Poison," Mohammed asserted. "He was poisoned. I saw him eating the figs."

I'd seen it, too, Dr. Grissard and Mustaf eating the figs together. But this memory only served to confuse me more. What part could poison have played in the doctor's death, in his self-proclaimed murder?

It would be several days before I had all the evidence in my possession and could calmly start to unravel this almost supernatural mystery.

(1) Who killed Dr. Grissard? (2) How was it done? (3) What was the original motive?

If you've already solved this mystery, check the Solution on p. 138.
To discover additional clues, turn to Gathering Evidence on p. 115.

HISTORICAL NOTES ON
EGYPTIAN TOMBS & THE PHARAOH'S CURSE

ALTHOUGH THERE WAS no curse etched over the entrance to Tutankhamen's tomb, such curses were not uncommon. One authentic curse reads as follows: "As for anyone who shall enter this tomb in his impurity, I shall wring his neck as I would a bird's."

It was Lord Carnarvon's strange death, five months after the tomb's opening, that sparked the legend. Doctors thought it might have been the result of an infection caused by an insect bite on his left cheek. Two years later, when the King Tut mummy was finally unwrapped, a similar mark was said to have been found on the body's left cheek.

By 1929, the press had attributed ten more strange and premature deaths to the pharaoh's curse, including one suicide. Lord Westbury, whose son had earlier died "from the curse," left the following note before jumping to his own death: "I really cannot stand any more horrors and hardly see what good I am going to do here, so I am making my exit."

By 1935, the number of so-called victims had reached twenty-one.

Was there really a curse? Were the deaths all coincidental? Or could it have been a combination of coincidence and a disease accidentally unearthed by the explorers?

In a 1999 study from the University of Leipzig, Dr. Gotthard Kramer suggested that some of the fatalities might have been caused by ancient spores. While analyzing the remains of 40 Egyptian mummies, Kramer found several potentially deadly mold spores, microorganisms that can survive for thousands of years.

Until the very end, Howard Carter was harassed by spiritualists, each with a theory on how to remove the curse hanging over his head. His death finally came in 1939—from natural causes.

THE TICKERTAPE
SUICIDE

New York City, 1929

I T WAS THE MORNING AFTER Black Tuesday, with the makings of a raw autumn day, but no one in New York was thinking about the weather. Some papers were already calling the day Red Wednesday in honor of the red ink that had been spilled. Or maybe it was in reference to blood. Rumor had it that stockbrokers were jumping out of their Wall Street windows.

Sergeant Vaile knew better. Brokers weren't jumping. Only one broker had jumped, and he'd hit the ground not on Wall Street, but on a dead-end alley some twenty yards off the fabled thoroughfare.

On that Wednesday morning, October 30, 1929, Vaile took the IRT down to the financial district to investigate this one lonely suicide. Odds were there'd be nothing to investigate, but his captain wanted to make sure. According to *The New York Sun,* $26 billion had been wiped out in one day. That's a lot of homicidal motive. Any stockbroker's death would have to be checked out.

Vaile arrived an hour before the markets opened to find the street deserted. Strands of tickertape and mounds of trash littered the pavement, like the aftermath of a battle. A familiar patrolman stood guard at the entrance to a narrow alley.

"O'Malley."

"Sarge."

"Where's our jumper?"

The patrolman pointed back into the dingy lane between office buildings. "Folks hardly ever go this way, so he could have been there for some time. A street bum found him about 7 A.M. We touched nothing but his wallet. Had to find out who he was."

"And who was he?"

"Casper Grant. He ran a small investment firm with his two partners. Grant, Baxter, and Slaughter. Jumped from his private office."

The body lay crumpled in the middle of the alley about halfway down its length. A middle-aged man in a custom-tailored suit. Vaile guessed that his spine had been broken. If he'd survived the fall, it hadn't been for long.

Two details immediately caught Vaile's attention. One was the expensive fountain pen sticking up out of the deceased's handkerchief pocket. Vaile checked the nib. Black ink. The other detail was easier to see. Lying on the man's ample stomach was a tickertape machine, the ribbon trailing out of it like a long, white tongue.

Sergeant Vaile checked the last time-stamp the machine had made: 4:28. "I thought the stock exchange closed at 3:30," he mumbled.

"It does." The patrolman was standing right over him, also eyeing the machine. "But there were so many shares traded yesterday the tickertapes were running two hours behind."

Vaile pushed himself to his feet. "You lose anything in this mess, O'Malley?"

"Not a cent. But my highfalutin brother-in-law, the butcher, he got wiped out." O'Malley stared at the body. "Looks like he wanted to take that ticker with him."

"Can you blame him?"

Before heading back toward the street, Vaile looked up. One side of the alley was a solid brick wall, perhaps ten stories of it. The other side was all one office tower, with windows starting on the third floor. Vaile scanned the column of windows above the body, going higher and higher. When his eyes hit the twelfth floor, he saw it. One of the windows was open.

"Anyone up there now?"

O'Malley nodded. "The secretary-receptionist. She came in early to try to organize things after yesterday. She's pretty broke up by the news."

When Sergeant Vaile opened the twelfth-floor door to Grant, Baxter, and Slaughter Investments, he found Maureen Richardson in the company of another patrolman. She was a young career girl, with bobbed hair like a flapper's, rouged cheeks, and a dress that revealed all of her shapely calves.

Vaile removed his hat, mouthed a few words of condolence, and then got down to business. "When did you last see Mr. Grant?"

"Well," she sobbed, "yesterday was a madhouse." As she continued speaking, more and more time elapsed between sobs. "Ever since Thursday, we've been trying to get our clients to cover their positions. But it was throwing good money after bad. Even I could see that.

"Yesterday it collapsed from the opening bell. Constant phone calls. People banging on the door, yelling. Finally, about 2:30, Mr. Grant couldn't take it anymore. He went into his office and asked me not to disturb him. No phone calls. Nothing."

Sergeant Vaile glanced around the reception room. Just inside the door were several comfortable chairs and a sofa. Beyond this waiting area was Miss Richardson's desk and telephone switchboard, a secretarial island that stood guard over three evenly-spaced doors, the three private offices of Grant, Baxter, and Slaughter.

"Was that the last you saw of Grant, when he asked not to be disturbed?"

"Yes, sir. The others kept taking calls and making calls. Mr. Baxter came out of his office around 4:00 and went home. Mr.

Slaughter left fifteen minutes later. My boyfriend came by around 4:30. He works in the area. I knocked on Mr. Grant's door, but it was locked and he didn't answer. So I left." The sobs welled up again. "I had no idea he'd kill himself."

Vaile had her unlock Grant's door. This center office was spacious, with a view overlooking the roof of the building across the alley. Four doors opened onto the office—one to the reception area, one to a small bathroom, one directly into Slaughter's office, and the other into Baxter's. On the desk was a suicide note written shakily in black ink. There were no fountain pens on the desk. The deceased must have taken his only one out the window with him. The room's only inkwell was nearly empty.

The only real surprise in the room was the tickertape machine. There it sat on its pedestal, completely wired, with yards of printed tape spewing from its jaws. Vaile reacted with a shiver. Maybe it was the breeze. He moved to the window and, using his handkerchief, closed it.

Lawrence Baxter was the first partner to arrive at work. Sergeant Vaile broke the news personally, then followed Baxter into his office for an interview. The first thing Vaile noticed was Baxter's own tickertape machine sitting in the middle of the room. "Why would Casper Grant kill himself?" he asked.

"Why not?" Baxter replied. "He was a bankrupt man. And he took dozens of others with him. You see, Casper was a big booster of buying stocks on margin." His voice adopted a professorial tone. "A margin is a loan. Instead of buying one share for a thousand dollars, you put down ten percent and buy ten shares for the same thousand. When the stock goes up, you sell, pay off the loan, and make a profit. But when the stock falls 70 percent…"

Vaile knew all about margin buying. "Not only do you lose everything, but you still owe the loan."

"Right. Well, Casper founded this firm on margin buying. Slaughter and I were conservative, hard-nosed brokers until Grant got hold of us. Now we're ruined. Even Maureen. Grant talked our secretary into taking her mother's life savings and putting it on margin."

Baxter said he had last seen his partner when Grant went into his office around 2:30. "He didn't want to be disturbed. Frankly, I was too busy with my own problems to worry about him."

Vaile asked Baxter for a sample of his handwriting and was handed an old draft of a letter. It was written in a neat, precise script, in brown ink.

When Oliver Slaughter arrived, Sergeant Vaile went through the same routine. Again, he found a tickertape machine. As for Slaughter's handwriting sample, it was dark blue, loose, and sloppy.

"You want a sample of Miss Richardson's writing?" O'Malley asked.

"Sure. Why don't you get it?" Sergeant Vaile watched as the eager patrolman exited to the reception area. "Mr. Slaughter, tell me about yesterday."

"Well, Baxter and I were in our offices, trying to contain the damage. We had an associate working the exchange floor. There were three or four stocks we were heavily invested in. Every few minutes, he would phone us. By the afternoon, that was the only way of staying up-to-date. Things were changing so fast."

Like Baxter and the secretary, Slaughter hadn't seen or heard from the deceased after 2:30. "I tried telephoning him, but the call had to go through Maureen, and she wouldn't put anybody through."

"He didn't want to be disturbed."

"That's what she said. I tried my connecting door to his office, but it was locked from his side."

Vaile returned to the dead man's office to find Officer O'Malley staring out the window and scratching his head. "I wonder why no one on the floors below noticed a man falling by their windows."

"I guess they were all busy with other things, like losing

millions of dollars." Vaile joined him at the window. "You get the secretary's handwriting?"

O'Malley handed him a piece of paper. The sample was in pencil, which was pretty much what Vaile expected. He hadn't seen a regular pen or an inkwell at her station. And fountain pens were men's utensils...and expensive.

"Thanks." He slipped it in his pocket. "O'Malley, check out this line of offices. See if anyone's missing a tickertape machine."

The patrolman looked confused. "Tickertape? What's the matter?"

"The machine on our victim is unaccounted for."

O'Malley paused and blinked. "What do you mean, victim? I thought this was a suicide."

"Nah, someone pushed him. I just gotta check a few things before I can make an arrest."

(1) How did Vaile know it was murder? (2) Who killed Casper Grant? (3) What clue points to the killer?

If you've already solved this mystery, check the Solution on p. 139.

To discover additional clues, turn to Gathering Evidence on p. 116.

HISTORICAL NOTES ON THE WALL STREET CRASH

THE 1920S WAS a decade of expansion and unbounded optimism. America had emerged from World War I as an economic powerhouse, facing what most thought was a limitless future.

The technology of the time, which centered around new uses for electricity, helped create a booming consumer economy. People were enthralled by electric washing machines, toasters, and machine-made clothes that looked hand-sewn but cost just a fraction. New innovations in credit, like paying on the installment plan, only fed this consumer buying spree.

The U.S. stock market reflected this phenomenon.

Financial speculation had once been the pastime of the rich. By 1925, that changed. People from all walks of life started buying stocks, confident that, no matter how much they paid, the price would only go higher.

Then early in 1929, the economy started to cool. Factories, which only a year earlier couldn't build appliances fast enough, were starting to stockpile their unsold goods.

For over a month, the stock market faltered and sputtered. Little new money was coming in.

The first traumatic day was October 24, 1929. Four billion dollars in value was lost. Banks and large investors stepped in, buying up "bargain" stocks and trying to reverse the panic.

On Monday, things turned bad again. And on Tuesday, October 29, Black Tuesday, disaster began with the opening bell and didn't stop.

Investors, large and small, stormed Wall Street, demanding their money. Fights broke out, and the police had to be called in. Brokers wandered the streets dazed as stocks plummeted 40 percent.

There are no records of any Wall Street suicides on that harrowing day. But Black Tuesday was only the start. President Herbert Hoover continued to promise America that "prosperity is just around the corner." But the market kept falling. By 1932, stocks had lost 89 percent of their value. Banks that had invested their customers' savings in stocks found themselves going bankrupt by the hundreds.

The crash was a catalyst that helped send the world into the Great Depression, an economic tailspin that would hurt or destroy millions of lives. One-third of American men became unemployed, with no Social Security or unemployment benefits to ease the pain. It would take the industrial needs of World War II to finally put the nation back to work.

As for the battered stock market, it did not return to its pre-crash heights until November, 1954.

THE MAN IN CABIN 16

Over the Atlantic, 1937

*J*ACK PAULING WASN'T A SPY. He was a junior attaché with the U.S. Embassy in Berlin, twenty-four years old, and wet behind the ears. Despite the excitement of the times, Jack was always given the dullest of jobs, setting schedules, holding meetings with his equally junior counterparts in the German government. But when word leaked out that Chancellor Hitler was sending a top courier from Berlin to Washington with secret papers, sensible, dull Jack was the one chosen to pursue him. "There's no one else," the ambassador said bluntly as he personally gave him the orders. "You must intercept those papers—at any cost."

The world was still at a tenuous peace as Jack tailed his courier across Germany to an airfield near Frankfurt. Jack watched his quarry board a zeppelin bound for the States. Passage on the lighter-than-air ship was expensive—$405 in U.S. dollars, he calculated, the price of a small car—but his orders were explicit, and the flight was only half full. Jack booked one of the remaining cabins and hurried on board. The date was May 3, 1937. In three days, this airship, the *Hindenburg*, would be landing in Lakehurst, New Jersey.

Jack did his best to blend in with the crowd. The bedroom cabins were tiny, but the observation lounge was comfortable and the service impeccable. The airship crew, decked out in

perfectly fitting brown uniforms, easily outnumbered the guests.

When the tow ropes were released, the *Hindenburg* slowly drifted up into the clouds. In the cramped two decks, everyone soon grew familiar with everyone else. More than once, the courier, Rudolph Lang, eyed Jack curiously.

"He recognizes me," Jack thought. "He must have seen me earlier. On the train from Berlin or maybe following him in the streets."

Late on that first night, as the *Hindenburg* floated majestically over the Atlantic, Jack followed Lang into the nearly empty lounge. Lang crossed to a far corner of the narrow room. "Heil," a voice said in a soft greeting. Jack could see a man's arm raised in a Nazi salute from a hidden chair. Someone was there, just out of Jack's line of sight.

"Heil, Heil," Lang answered in an amused tone.

"You think it's funny?" the voice growled back. "This American is after you. I would take the papers myself, but I have a rendezvous in Boston. Legally, that pouch is the property of Germany and can't be touched. But once in America...I warn you, Lang. Do not become a liability."

Jack slithered behind a bulkhead. But the drone of the propellers prevented him from hearing anything more.

For the next two days, Jack did his best to keep an eye on Lang as he kept himself out of sight. It wasn't easy. Fritzy, one of the cabin attendants, always seemed to be nearby, offering a drink or wondering out loud why Jack was loitering in shadowy doorways.

The last morning arrived with an annoying development. Thunderstorms were preventing them from landing on time. The captain announced a 12-hour delay, then treated the passengers to a floating tour of the New York skyline. As they passed over Manhattan the ship came within a hundred feet of the spire of the Empire State Building, a spire that had been designed, but never used, as a mooring mast for these airships.

Late that afternoon, Jack was walking down a corridor when he heard a soft cry of pain and a muffled groan. It had come from the cabin he'd just passed. Cabin 16, Rudolph Lang's.

The junior attaché turned back, his heart in his throat, and knocked on the cabin door. No answer. The curtains were drawn on the window and the door was locked. Jack checked the empty corridor, then ran to the outer door and threw it open. He was standing in a hallway by a stairwell, both of them empty. And then a shadow and the sound of footsteps on stairs. Fritzy was wandering up from B Deck. "There's an emergency," Jack shouted at the cabin attendant. "Hurry!"

Jack pulled Fritzy in the corridor, babbling to him in broken German, trying to explain. Just as they reached Cabin 16, the *Hindenburg*'s resident doctor came strolling down from the other end of the corridor. "What is the matter?" he inquired.

Jack stated the facts, at the same time urging Fritzy to hurry and use his passkey. When the door finally opened, the three men peered into the dimly lit cabin and saw Rudolph Lang, German state courier, lying on his narrow bunk, a knife protruding from his bloody chest.

The doctor pushed his way past the others and knelt by the motionless man. "Dead," he whispered. "Come in for a minute. Close the door." The room could barely accommodate the men and the corpse.

The *Hindenburg*'s physician immediately took charge. "I will inform the captain. Leave the body as it is. You will lock the door, Fritzy. Inform the other attendants not to open this cabin, not for anyone. You, sir." He turned to Jack. "You must not tell a soul. The captain will handle this his own way." The doctor, it seemed to Jack, was more concerned about the bad publicity for the Third Reich's luxury airship than about the murder itself.

Helpless, Jack let himself be pushed out of the cabin. Fritzy locked the door and, like a true Prussian, went about his duties. Jack returned to his own cabin to think. What should he do? Was his mission over, now that Lang was dead? No, he decided. Of course not. He must recover the papers.

Jack was just leaving his cabin when a series of three long whistles played on the intercom. As on any ship, this was a well-known signal. Everyone, passengers and crew alike, was to gather immediately in the observation lounge.

The long lounge was packed with eager faces. The threat of thunderstorms was over. In a few minutes, they would make a final pass over Coney Island, across Brooklyn to Manhattan, then on to New Jersey. The captain was in full uniform. The entire crew, except for the first mate, were standing in tight, neat rows. As the captain thanked the guests and explained the disembarking procedures, Jack idly counted the crew. Sixty. He counted again. Sixty, not counting the first mate who was manning the wheel. Number of passengers? Thirty-five, not counting the corpse in Cabin 16.

When the captain dismissed the meeting, many of the passengers stayed by the windows. But not Jack. He knew what he had to do—get into Cabin 16. And he'd already picked out the man to help.

A cabin attendant, one that Jack had never seen before, had stood shyly at the back. "He probably doesn't know which cabin I'm in," Jack mused. "With any luck, I can persuade him that I lost my key."

The attendant was a gruff man, middle-aged, with great sideburns and a waxed mustache that must have been all the rage during the late Great War.

"Excuse me," Jack said in his best German as he button-holed the shy man. "I've locked myself out of my cabin. Can you help me?"

The attendant identified himself as Günther. He was brisk and solicitous, until he learned that the cabin in question was number 16. "*Ach, nein.* We are under orders not to allow anyone in that cabin. I don't know why. Perhaps I can talk to the captain."

"No," Jack said as he fell into retreat. "Don't bother. I'll figure something out."

Jack did figure something out. From the smoking room he stole a metal pipe cleaner and then, after several tries, managed to jimmy open the locked cabin.

But inside there was no body. No body, no blood, no hint of the murder scene. And worst of all, no trace of the leather pouch containing the papers Rudolph Lang had been carrying to America.

Jack stood in Cabin 16, mulling over his predicament. The transatlantic voyage was almost over. The *Hindenburg* now hovered over its mooring masts. In the distance, he could hear orders being shouted down to the ground crew.

And then it happened, the terrific, deafening explosion. The floor under Jack's feet tilted back. The room was falling. Everything was falling. Jack ran into the corridor, and was instantly overwhelmed by the smoke. And then, in a whoosh, came the flames.

Only in the aftermath did Jack understand the enormity of it. In less than a minute, an unexplained explosion and fire had destroyed the huge airship, killing dozens of crew and passengers.

Jack emerged with only superficial burns. Sitting among the other stunned survivors in the customs shed, he was, like them, awaiting the ambulances that would transport them to hospitals. As the confusion subsided, Jack looked around for his German acquaintances. The doctor, he saw, was alive. Fritzy had also survived, along with the other attendant, Günther.

Despite his painful burns, Jack focused his mind. He had to discover the truth before everyone dispersed, and his chance of securing the papers was gone forever.

Jack located the police captain in charge. He explained who he was and showed his credentials. "Before anyone from the *Hindenburg* leaves this building, I need to get some answers."

The captain quickly grasped the situation and pledged his full cooperation.

(1) Who killed Rudolph Lang? (2) Who is the other German agent? (3) Who now has the secret papers?

If you've already solved this mystery, check the Solution on p. 140.
To discover additional clues, turn to Gathering Evidence on p. 117.

HISTORICAL NOTES ON ZEPPELINS & AIRSHIPS

AROUND THE YEAR 1900, Count von Zeppelin designed the lighter-than-air ship that would later bear his name, a rigid, motorized, cigar-shaped vehicle lifted by helium.

Throughout the 1920s and 1930s, the Zeppelin Company of Germany developed these airships as a form of global transportation. In an age when airplanes were dangerous, cramped, and limited in range, the zeppelin was heralded as the passenger carrier of the future. The *Graf Zeppelin* in the late twenties and early thirties became a potent symbol of Germany's technological superiority.

When the *Hindenburg* was christened in 1936, it represented the next step. It stood 16 stories tall and 808 feet long, only $78^1/_2$ feet shorter than the *Titanic*. It still holds the record as the largest flying object ever built.

The *Hindenburg* differed from earlier designs, in that the passenger area was not in an attached gondola but was built into the hull. The living space included 25 cabins, a dining room, a lounge with a baby grand piano, a reading room, showers, a kitchen, a bar, a smoking room, plus full facilities for the crew. The two promenades were equipped with windows that could open.

Because of the Zeppelin Company's ties to the Nazi government, the United States, the world's only supplier of helium, refused to sell them the nonflammable gas. This forced the *Hindenburg*'s owners to use flammable hydrogen. They set new fire precautions in place. Matches, flashbulbs, and lighters were removed from passengers' luggage. The smoking room was fireproofed with extra air pressure to keep out any stray hydrogen. The only cigarette lighter was chained to a table in the middle of the room.

No one knows the cause of the *Hindenburg* explosion and fire. Was it an atmospheric fluke left over from the thunderstorms? A careless spark? One theory pins the blame on the flammable varnish used to tighten the ship's outer skin. According to this theory, even if the *Hindenburg* had been filled with helium, it would still have burned.

The *Hindenburg* disaster spelled the end of passenger dirigibles. The *Graf Zeppelin II*, then under construction in Germany, was dismantled. Within a few years, airplanes could make the transatlantic crossing without refueling. For the next six decades, no new dirigibles were built. (Modern-day blimps are much smaller and not rigid. Like balloons, they take their shape from the gas inside them.)

Today, the Zeppelin Company is once again in the airship business. There are currently three in service, transporting sightseers in Germany and ferry passengers in Japan.

THE CORNER OF HOLLYWOOD & CRIME

Hollywood, May 18, 1940

HE BIG NEWS OF THE day should have been the earthquake. Things in the nearby Imperial Valley had started rumbling a few minutes after 8:30 P.M. and Charles Richter was rating the disaster as a 6.9 on his new scale, though no one had any idea of what that meant.

This was Hollywood, after all. And notwithstanding a few cracked buildings and bridges, people had more important things on their minds. Only a handful of reporters turned up at Caltech to interview Professor Richter. Five times as many made their way to the hillside mansion of Marian Doral to witness the mysterious press conference that the legendary star had scheduled for the provocative hour of 11:45 P.M.

Security was always tight at the Doral estate. In years past, many of these same reporters had been stopped by the vigilant guards or chased by the pack of German shepherds that roamed just inside the high walls. But tonight, they were ushered inside the massive gates and escorted toward the mansion itself.

"What do you know?" whispered a stringer from *The New York Times*. He was pointing to the swimming pool cantilevered over the Hollywood Hills. "I guess even Marian Doral can't keep out an earthquake." They focused their cameras on the dramatic fissure in the empty pool's blue-tiled side. Flashbulbs popped.

"Ten to one, this is about the divorce," hissed the reporter from *Variety*.

Rumors had been running rampant. Nearly a year earlier, Marian Doral had wed Ben McMasters and, in the process, gone against good judgment and the opinion of everyone close to her. It was common knowledge, at least within the movie industry, that the star and the polo player had embarked on one of the most tempestuous marriages in a town hardly known for stable relationships.

Cameras were confiscated at the door and the reporters were crowded into the cavernous entry hall. At 11:50 P.M., Marian's manager and brother, Dexter Doral, stepped out onto the dimly lit balcony twenty feet above the sea of heads.

"Thank you for coming." Everyone liked Dexter. He had the Doral good looks but was down-to-earth and friendly, even to journalists. If Dexter happened to be totally dependent on his younger sister for employment...well, people seemed willing to overlook that.

"Marian was so looking forward to talking to you," he announced. A groan floated up from the crowd. Did this mean the box-office goddess wasn't going to make an appearance? For someone who made her living in the public eye, Marian Doral could be annoyingly private. "The pain of tonight's announcement has affected her so deeply..."

Dexter stopped as a bedroom door eased open behind him. The entry hall fell into a hush as a stunning woman, her face framed in a halo of golden hair, stepped out from the shadows. Her makeup, as usual, was perfect. But there was a tiredness and a sadness in her face. "Ben and I are getting a divorce," she said softly and simply. "Dexter?" she added, then stepped back and let her brother take over.

The reporters gazed sympathetically, pens poised over their pads. Ever since the last days of silent films, Marian Doral had been America's siren, a homegrown answer to Garbo and Dietrich. A nation of moviegoers still loved the gently aging actress, even though they'd stopped going to her movies. Her last four films had proved disappointing, and there were the usual rumors of depression, alcohol, and pills.

"The papers were filed months ago," Dexter explained. "The divorce becomes final at midnight. That was the reason Marian invited you here at this unusual hour, to share the occasion with her."

A barrage of eager questions shot up from the floor. But before the fragile woman in the shadows could answer any of them, another voice, louder and more demanding, erupted from behind. The news writers turned on their heels and saw Ben McMasters in the doorway, a sweaty, apologetic security guard at his side.

"What do you mean, keeping me out of my own house?" he demanded. The reporters closest to him could smell the booze.

Dexter stepped forward protectively. "In five minutes, it won't be your house. This has all been worked out with the lawyers, Ben."

"I don't want a divorce," the handsome playboy pleaded. "Marian, please. I never wanted your money or your fame. I want you."

The reporters parted like the Red Sea as Ben dashed toward the staircase. The star on the balcony looked confused, almost frightened. Before Marian's estranged husband could reach the top of the stairs, she had fled back into her bedroom suite.

Ben pounded on the door, begging her to let him in. Dozens of pencils scratched out the dramatic details, and it might have almost seemed like a publicity stunt, except for the fact that there would be no romantic, last-minute reconciliation. The clock struck midnight, and the couple was officially divorced.

Dexter answered several questions and then the bedroom door opened again. Ben's face fell as he recognized Brenda Doral, Marian's older sister. The women were so different, not so much in appearance—Brenda was an inch shorter, with darker coloring and shorter hair—but in personality and temperament. The cold, efficient Brenda stood in the doorway. "Marian refuses to see you, Ben. Please leave with the members of the press."

In the next morning's papers, the divorce made bigger headlines than the Imperial Valley earthquake with its eight deaths and millions in damage. The afternoon papers had even bigger headlines, no longer screaming about Marian's divorce, but about her death, just hours after the scene on the balcony. The star's body had been discovered by her devoted secretary, Harriet Brown.

"Miss Doral usually takes a late-night bath," Harriet told the police in her statement. "At 6 A.M. I always arrive in her bedroom with her coffee. We discuss her correspondence for half an hour before she heads off to MGM for makeup and costume. I knew she didn't sleep last night. But I never change the routine, not without direct orders. When I came into the bedroom this morning, I could see her bed hadn't been slept in. I called out for Miss Doral and when she didn't answer, I entered her bathroom. The tub was full, the water was cold, and the bubbles had all died down. I could see her clearly, her head under the water, her hair floating all around. It was horrible."

Officer Marvin Westlake spotted the bottle of pills on the edge of the bathtub and the half-empty bottle of Jack Daniels bobbing at the far end.

"It's a deep tub," Westlake told his partner who was looking, not listening. "The sides are steep and slippery. It's going to take the coroner to figure out what happened. Was it suicide? Or an accident? Did she slip and get knocked unconscious? The water's pretty high. Maybe she got knocked woozy and didn't have the strength to pull herself out. Hey, stop ogling; that's indecent."

"You're ogling, too," the partner defended himself. "Marian Doral," he added in awe, finally tearing his eyes away. "Just hours after her divorce went through. I wonder if we'll ever find out what really happened here."

(1) How did Marian die? (2) Who covered up the truth and how? (3) What was the motive?

If you've already solved this mystery, check the Solution on p. 141. To discover additional clues, turn to Gathering Evidence on p. 118.

HISTORICAL NOTES ON EARTHQUAKES

THE FIRST RECORDED earthquake in California was in the Los Angeles area in 1769, chronicled by the Gaspar de Portola expedition.

No scientific way of measuring an earthquake existed until the 1890s when John "Earthquake" Milne invented the seismograph machine. But even with the seismograph, there was no way of comparing the intensity of quakes, not until 1935, when Charles Richter developed a set of logarithms now known as the Richter scale. Feeling that there should be a distinctive word to describe the strength of an earthquake—like the word *watt* for electricity or *horsepower* for engines—Richter borrowed a term from the world of astronomy, *magnitude.* One of the first events measured on the scale was the one in our story.

Contrary to popular belief, the Richter scale is not based on a scale of 1 to 10. Each point on the scale corresponds to a tenfold increase. A 6-point quake, for instance, is ten times stronger than a 5-point quake.

The strongest quake ever recorded was in Chile in 1960 (9.5), while the deadliest is believed to be a 1556 disaster in China, killing over 830,000.

TWO SWORDSMEN
OF VERONA

Fictional History, circa 1300

THE LOVERS HAD DIED JUST three years earlier. At the time
it was thought that the tragic deaths of Romeo and
Juliet would help end the feud that had plagued the
noble houses for so many decades, and for a while, this proved
to be the case. Escalus, princely emissary of the Doge, was so
moved by their deaths that he ordered a truce and a yearlong
period of contrition and penance.

The sorrowful families joined forces to mourn. Lord
Montague built an impressive funereal monument so that the
young husband and wife, once divided by clan hatred, might
now be united, awaiting the resurrection. But this loving
tribute to his son was the very wedge that began to destroy
the fragile peace.

Lady Capulet was young and seemingly docile. The second
wife of Lord Capulet, she had been devoted to her daughter and
in some part blamed herself for Juliet's death. To inter a
deceased couple in the vault of the husband's family was an
incontestable right. No one could oppose it. But seeing her sole
daughter taken from her own family tomb and buried among the
despised Montagues was more than Lady Capulet's nature could
bear. And so, almost from the day of the funeral that was meant
to end their strife, the seeds of discord were sown once again.

The feud recommenced with all the subtlety of Machiavelli.
Genial smiles turned begrudging, then became frowns.

Greetings on the street went unreturned. Social snubs and whispered insults escalated at a snail's pace, unnoticed by the prince until the situation had once again gone beyond his poor powers to correct.

The roiling tempers came to a boil on a hot afternoon in June when Lords Capulet and Montague met in a public square. No others were present, so it was impossible to determine exactly how the fight began. But rapiers were drawn, and by the time citizens and courtiers came within sight, Lord Capulet lay wounded on the cobblestones, his hand clutched to the thick leather jerkin popularly worn at the time.

"My sword barely touched him," Lord Montague claimed to the onlookers who were already murmuring and starting to take sides.

"A palpable hit," protested Capulet and clutched his chest in agony.

Within minutes, Prince Escalus arrived in the square, his face dark with anger. If the offenders had been any less than the patriarchs of their houses, he would have banished them on the spot. But such a decree on two such men would only fuel the flames between the clans.

"Bring Lord Capulet to the Castelvecchio," he ordered. "He will stay as my guest until this fever of hatred is broken. Lady Capulet." He saw that the stricken man's wife had already arrived on the scene. "Call a surgeon for your husband and come with us."

"No surgeon," Lord Capulet insisted. "Lady Capulet can attend to me herself."

The prince regarded the young noblewoman. "I am well trained in the healing of wounds," she explained modestly. "Life among the Montagues has rendered the Capulet women finer surgeons, and more trusted, than any others in Verona."

The prince granted them their whim. Lady Capulet sent a servant running for bandages and ointments and a nightshirt, then gently supervised the loading of her husband onto a litter. She followed at a pace behind during the short walk to the prince's castle.

The royal household opened its doors for the injured lord. Candles were lit, a room was opened and aired, and Lady Capulet set about easing her husband into bed. She called for a pan of water, then dismissed the servants and set about dressing the wound herself.

That night, as the clock in the tower struck ten, Prince Escalus and his kinsman, Count Anselmo, paid a visit to Lord Capulet's bedside. The middle-aged nobleman lay pale and listless. "He'll live," Lady Capulet whispered comfortingly.

"For no reason, he assaulted me," rasped the injured man. "And he will try again. You must banish Montague."

The prince said nothing, but Count Anselmo bristled. The count's elder brother, Paris, had been killed on the same night as the lovers' suicide, murdered by Romeo, just feet away from the Capulet crypt. Anselmo blamed both families for his beloved brother's death. The renewing of the feud only served to anger him more. "How many more must die?" he demanded. "When will this madness end?"

"When we're all dead in our graves," hissed Capulet.

"Enough," said Prince Escalus. "You will be safe here until your body and temper are healed. Latch the doors and windows," he called to a servant. "Place a guard in the hallway. There will be no more killing."

The prince and count left the sickroom, followed shortly by Lady Capulet. An hour later, just as the clock in the tower struck eleven and a soft rain began to fall over Verona, Lady Capulet returned to the room. The guard in the hall unlocked the door and ushered her inside. It took only a minute to satisfy her concerns. "He's asleep," she reported to the guard, then walked down the hall to the chambers the prince had provided for her own use.

The tower clock struck the half-hour, 11:30. The shower had passed and the moon peered out from behind the clouds. Bertram, a captain in the guard, had just come off duty. He was walking by the west wing of the castle, carrying a full flagon of wine to the barracks, when he tripped over a sizable object. The flagon was tossed and his precious wine seeped into the wet ground. Bertram cursed. And then, by the moonlight, he saw the object: a middle-aged man dressed in a thick leather jerkin and pantaloons. The man lay face up, a rapier in his right hand. Bertram quickly recognized him as Lord Capulet. And he was dead.

Bertram didn't move the body. Instead, he knelt and gingerly unhooked the jerkin. He had heard of the disturbance to the civil peace today—all of Verona had heard—and his first thought was to examine the wound delivered earlier by Lord Montague. The bandage wrapped around the torso was soaked with blood. With gentle fingers, Bertram eased away the cloth and looked at the wound. It was rapier thin and deep. "How did he even live so long?" the guard marveled.

"What have you there, soldier?"

Bertram started and turned and found himself staring up at Prince Escalus and Count Anselmo. He leaped to attention. "Your grace, it's Lord Capulet. Dead from the Montague's wound."

"What was Capulet doing?..." Prince Escalus inspected the body and the rapier, then turned to see the loosely closed window in the west wing. "That was his sickroom. Why was the man out of doors, fully clothed, and with a sword?"

Count Anselmo was on his knees, his gloves off, feeling for any trace of life. "It's clear to me," he said, looking up, his face flushed with anger. "Not content with your decree of peace, Capulet rose from his sickbed and spirited himself out the window. He was on his way to deal with Montague when his wound tore open."

"He's not long dead," Bertram ventured. "Lady Capulet saw him in his chamber at eleven by the clock-tower bell, half an hour before I came to this spot and found him."

"Is it murder then?" asked Anselmo. "To die from a wound inflicted in a fight would place the fault with Lord Montague."

The prince shrugged. "Perhaps. And yet Capulet's own recklessness was as much the cause as Montague's rapier."

"Your grace," Bertram stammered. "If I may have your permission to examine the situation, I might shed some light on this."

Prince Escalus trusted his captain and had commented more than once that the young officer was bright, well beyond his station. "Very well," he assented. "You may examine what you like and question whom you will."

And with that, the prince turned and left the scene, followed by his kinsman Anselmo.

(1) Who was planning a murder? (2) Who was responsible for Lord Capulet's death? (3) What clue points to the guilty party?

If you've already solved this mystery, check the Solution on p. 142.

To discover additional clues, turn to Gathering Evidence on p. 119.

HISTORICAL NOTES ON
SHAKESPEARE'S ROMEO & JULIET

AS WAS THE case with many of Shakespeare's plays, *Romeo & Juliet* was adapted from earlier works of fiction: a moralistic poem based on an Italian novel based on a short story that was based on another novel set in Verona and featuring Romeo and Giulietta. The original plot, of a sleeping potion drunk by the heroine to avoid a bad marriage, can be traced back to a Greek story of the third century A.D.

The actual period of Shakespeare's play, a world of feuding clans and princely emissaries, is probably around 1300, when Verona was governed by the Doges of Venice.

Nowadays, the city of Verona has fostered a Romeo and Juliet circuit, featuring a walking tour of the couple's crypt, Romeo's house, and also Juliet's. This last structure, a museum to the fictional heroine, dates back to the correct period and had been home to the Cappello family, a close-enough approximation of Capulet. The Juliet bedroom even features a picturesque balcony facing a courtyard. What many tourists don't realize is that this famous balcony was built only recently, to make the house better conform to the Shakespeare play.

GATHERING
EVIDENCE

"Fall of a Social Climber"

INTERVIEW WITH NORTEO

Moderatus found the Nubian slave leaving the master's quarters, a cloth bundle under his arm. Moderatus followed his friend to the front portal, then stopped him. Norteo jumped, his nerves as raw as a fresh wound. "What is in the bundle?"

Norteo laughed nervously. "The actor," he blurted out. "Master Eppides forgot his belongings from the bath. I was about to return them."

"Let me see," Moderatus said.

Norteo undid the loose knot, exposing the dinner toga Eppides had worn at the feast. Moderatus unfurled it and immediately noticed a greasy food stain on the side, ruining the entire garment. Moderatus shook his head. People should be more careful.

Tucked inside the robe, Norteo had placed the actor's cleaning strigil. "Is this everything?" Moderatus asked.

"That's all he had with him," Norteo said. "And I didn't stain the toga. It was already like that."

FOLLOW ACHILIUS

Moderatus was excited at the prospect of earning his freedom. But what if Achilius himself had done the poisoning? No, Moderatus decided. It must be someone else. It must be.

The slave's heart sank, however, when he caught sight of the young master out behind the house. He was holding a shovel and standing over a freshly dug hole. Moderatus approached cautiously, stopping beside Achilius and peering down in. A hunting dog lay inside the makeshift grave. Dead. "My father's favorite hound," Achilius explained. "We found him curled in a corner."

Dogs had been known to expire from grief at the death of their masters. But in this case Moderatus doubted it.

INTERVIEW WITH LADY SABBINA

Moderatus found his mistress in the rear garden, a lone torch from the dinner party illuminating the ground around her. For the first time that evening, Moderatus looked at the flowers laid along the path. It didn't surprise him to find a patch of yellow buttercups missing from the flowerbed, torn up by their roots.

"Moderatus, remind me in the morning." Lady Sabbina didn't bother to look up at her dead husband's slave. "We must go to the market. They say there are new slaves arriving from Gaul. I need someone to take Norteo's place when I set him free."

To review the most vital clues, see Deductive Reasoning on p. 122.

"THE CHALICE OF CANA"

EXAMINE THE BODY

A sympathetic friar allowed Jean to pay his last respects. Friar Germain's body was laid out in the monastery chapel, in the same state in which it had been found. Jean was surprised by the lack of blood on the dead man's robe. Even around the stomach, where the crude iron dagger had been inserted, there were few traces of blood.

EXAMINE THE TREASURY

Bishop Faisant himself granted permission for Jean to enter the treasury. A priest kept an eye on the blacksmith as he toured the sodden, rubble-filled room. On all four sides it was lined with a shelf holding the church's treasured books and icons. In the center was a small, altarlike table covered with red felt. The finger bones of John the Baptist were still on display in their bulky reliquary. Next to this reliquary was a circular outline, nearly dry, where the precious chalice had once rested.

INTERVIEW WITH THE BISHOP

"I had an appointment with Pierre of Chantilly. But it had been set back until noon—to allow me to meet the ship from Scandinavia. Perhaps Pierre hadn't been informed. I was onboard the ship when the lightning struck. I arrived just as my men broke down the treasury door. I remember poor Friar Germain lying there, his hands clutched to his chest. There was a sizable hole in the roof pierced through by parts of the spire. The stonecutter was still on the roof, keeping guard until we arrived."

To review the most vital clues, see Deductive Reasoning on p. 122.

"DEAD MAN'S CHEST"

EXAMINE THE MONEY CHEST

The chest was old and worn and far from airtight. These days, it wasn't used to hold anything. John knew this, for he had once looked inside as, he supposed, had many others. Rooster kept it close to the doorway, but out of sight from the tavern room. John looked into the chest and was surprised to see the spatter of blood on all the interior sides.

EXAMINE THE STOREROOM DOOR

The method by which Captain Will, or his body, had come into the tavern was John's biggest mystery. He examined the bolt on the storeroom door. It had been swollen from the humidity and he could see it had recently been forced open, then re-closed. There were no cobwebs connected to the bolt, although elsewhere in the room, the webs were everywhere.

INSPECT JOHN'S MEDICINE CABINET

Like most of the loose contents, John Leftum's recently plundered medicine cabinet had been removed before the ship was careened on its side. The cabinet was valuable to no one but him, yet someone had been rummaging through it. John held up each bottle of thick glass and quickly determined what was missing: the mandrake root powder. Mandrake root was known to have many extraordinary properties, including that of a strong sleeping potion. Who, John wondered, had been in need of a sleeping potion?

To review the most vital clues, see Deductive Reasoning on p. 123.

"DEATH IN THE SERENE REPUBLIC"

EXAMINE THE BODY

Giorgio used his authority to take the dead woman to a physician in the Jewish quarter, a man undeterred by the Catholic proscription against mutilating the dead. "The water in the lungs means she drowned," the old doctor reported. "The stomach is empty of food, meaning she hadn't eaten for at least four hours. There are bruises on the arms and legs consistent with a drowning of this sort."

SUICIDE WITNESS

"I saw the woman on the bridge. I work in the palazzo next to Ca' Contini and I recognized Signora Contini's gown right away. She was very agitated. It would have been out of place for me to approach her. I wish I had. When she removed the silver mask, I caught a glimpse of her face and her hair. And then she jumped."

INTERVIEW WITH HOUSEHOLD SERVANT

"Signora Contini knew of her husband's affair. I remember three months ago, when the palazzo's boat slips were being repaired. The signora found a love note from Maria Garda. So angry she was. She ran down to the outside dock with a hammer and knocked a hole in the master's gondola."

Giorgio asked when she had last seen the victim. "I helped

dress the Signora for the Golden Ball. Then she excused us. All the servants left for the night. I was at a party in Piazza San Marco when I heard the news."

To review the most vital clues, see Deductive Reasoning on p. 123.

"A CLOCKWORK MURDER"

LOCATION OF SUSPECTS

The old watchman hobbled to the small, unlatched window and threw it open. The moon came out from behind a cloud, throwing light across the winding alleys. The town below seemed asleep, but there was still movement reflected against the gray cobblestones. In a lane behind the Brown Bear Inn, Herman Braun was lighting his long white clay pipe. To the left, Mayor Birchenstock sat on a boulder in his garden as if reluctant to go in to face Dame Birchenstock. And on the steps of St. Mary's sat Marta Braun, rocking back and forth, her head buried in her hands.

EXAMINING THE BODY

"You're young and already greasy," Hans said, pointing to a mark on the right sleeve of Johann's velvet *brezon*. "You go down."

Johann obeyed, climbing gingerly down among the cogs and levers. It would take more than one man to free the twisted body from the metal and wood clockworks. The young herdsman's eye rested on the bloody gash. The skull itself had been battered in by what looked like one severe blow. Carl Jurgen had been killed quickly by someone with strength. The body had then been pushed over the edge and down into the churning gears. But why?

SCENE OF THE CRIME

As Johann clambered up out of the mechanism, Hans glanced around the clock room. A stool lay on its side and the wood floor showed the scuff marks of boots. Lying in a far corner was a mallet, the largest of several used in the clock-making trade. A red stain decorated its head and smears of blood dripped down to the handle.

To review the most vital clues, see Deductive Reasoning on p. 124.

"A SNAKE IN THE ASH PILE"

HECTOR'S WHEREABOUTS

Doc Maynard found Hector at the flap of his small canvas tent. Doc sat down on a stump and knocked the ashes from his pipe. "Hector, where were you all morning?"

The ex-slave seemed nervous. "I was with Mrs. Mabel. We packed up the wheelbarrow with pies. Then we went around the camps, selling 'em. After the snakebite, when you took Mr. Jesse away, I stayed around their cabin, like she told me. The stove was full of ashes, so I emptied it out. I carried a couple buckets down to the ash pile. Then I came back here to keep guard on the camp."

SEARCH FOR SNAKE

Doc Maynard arrived just as Abner and Hector were looking through the brush by Jesse's cabin. "We're searching for that rattler," Abner said, "although I don't think there ever really was..." And then his foot hit something. It was a small wooden box with holes punched in the top. Abner opened it gingerly. It was empty except for a few scaly inches of a shiny skin.

"I'll be hog-tied," he said in surprise. "Snake skin."

SEARCH AROUND THE CABIN

"Look at what Hector and I found." Abner had brought Doc Maynard to the edge of the woods, a dozen yards from where Johnny had been seen cutting open Jesse's leg. He pointed to the ash pile. "There was a hole in the ashes. Hector stuck his hand in and came out with this." It was a glass bottle with a cork stopper. "Someone must've pushed it down in there with a stick."

Doc Maynard removed the cork and sniffed the brown liquid. "Nicotine," he said. "Probably from boiled cigarette stubs. Touch it to an open wound and you'll be dead in fifteen minutes."

To review the most vital clues, see Deductive Reasoning on p. 124.

"FIRE & RAIN"

EXAMINE THE VICTIM'S GUN

Judge Cramdon smelled the barrel, cracked open the cylinder, and then passed it to Walter Root for inspection. "The gun was recently fired," Root confirmed. "And two bullet chambers are empty. Were there two shots fired?"

"Yes," Cramdon replied. "Close together. Perhaps the echo confused you."

EXAMINE THE CRIME SCENE

The others watched suspiciously as the Frenchman walked across the broken window glass. "Something is missing here, no?" He pointed to a leather folder open on the *Tribune* editor's desk. The ribbons had been untied and the contents, if there had been any, were nowhere to be seen.

He continued his tour of the room, stopping at the far wall. A patch of hazy sunlight illuminated a small dark indentation. The French artist took a pallet knife from his pocket and used it to pry a bullet from the hole. "There must've been two shots. The second bullet is here." It was a 0.36-caliber shot, matching the kind used in the Colt revolver.

CHECK THE OUTER DOOR

They had done all they could at the Johnson house. Judge Cramdon helped his wife into her coat, then threw on his own and grabbed his monogrammed umbrella from the hall stand. At the door, he stopped to examine the lock.

"One of those new spring locks," he observed. "It locks without a key. You draw the door shut and it can't be opened from the outside. That's how the killer got out of a locked house."

To review the most vital clues, see Deductive Reasoning on p. 125.

"THE RIPPER'S LAST VICTIM"

EXCERPT FROM THE REPORTER'S STORY

We heard no more of her desperate cries, only the sound of footsteps, several calm deliberate footsteps, as her foul attacker fled the scene. The echoes bounding off stone and brick made it difficult to ascertain the source of her shouts. But a sixth sense seemed to inform my companion, and he darted through an archway in search of his wife.

Her body lay halfway down the short lane, face up, her arms spread, imploring heaven to take her to a better world.

POLICE RECORDS

Ruth Tanner: Two arrests for lewd conduct and solicitation. On October 4, she was detained after an altercation with Mrs. Jillian Jones Wainwright at the entrance to Farrow's Music Hall. No charges were pressed.

Daryl "Danny" Wainwright: No criminal record. On August

14 and again on the afternoon of September 30, Wainwright was arrested for public drunkenness. On both occasions, he was detained overnight.

Amos Pickering: Served a one-year sentence for battery in the beating of Beadle John Wilcox, an officer of the court.

Ezekiel Braun: No criminal record in England.

POST MORTEM

"Death occurred from manual strangulation. Hand prints, probably those of a male, were found around her throat, thumbs in front and fingers curled around the neck, index fingers closest to the shoulders. The deceased's hands were raised to her throat area, in a state of rigor mortis."

To review the most vital clues, see Deductive Reasoning on p. 125.

"THE ECCENTRIC ALCHEMIST"

INTERVIEW WITH THE PORTER

"The man who rented the room was tall, like the dead man. He wore a beard and a hat pulled low, so I'm not positive it's the same man. He arrived several weeks ago with a single cheap suitcase, like the one in the corner. At the beginning, I saw him a fair amount, coming and going. But very little in the past few days. I don't remember anyone visiting him. But then I'm not always around, am I?"

THE BLOODHOUNDS' DISCOVERY

When Rolf returned to see the farmer, he was rewarded with a strange story. At first the bloodhounds pulled the farmer toward the manor house, the place where the man with the scarf had stayed. But eventually, the dogs picked up a new scent. It led them to a spot of freshly turned dirt by the edge of the woods.

The farmer showed Rolf what he had unearthed. There

were six golden statuettes, ornamented with jewels. "Are they real?" the farmer asked.

Rolf inspected them carefully. "They're forgeries," he replied. "Good forgeries. But the gold is fake; so are the jewels."

INTERVIEW WITH VACLAV

The coachman admitted that he had been the one to find the scarf and matchbook. "Right after you left us, I went into Herr Greenway's room and searched. I found those objects and handed them to the count. He was very excited and thankful. He gave me the rest of the day off and I went to the St. Vitus festival in the village."

To review the most vital clues, see Deductive Reasoning on p. 126.

"CURSE OF THE PHARAOH"

AUTOPSY RESULTS

On arriving in Luxor, we brought Grissard's body to the home of Dr. Warren-Height, a highly regarded physician, originally from Bristol. His examination confirmed what we suspected. Dr. Grissard had ingested poison, specifically, potassium cyanide. An examination of his intestines and stomach, however, revealed no trace of poison there.

INSPECTION OF THE COLLAPSED TUNNEL

On my return to the excavation site the next day, I inspected the collapsed tunnel and discovered the following: Behind the debris that killed Abdel Effendi were several small, perfectly preserved funerary statues, undoubtedly from the Tutankhamen tomb. My analysis of the tunnel structure revealed no weakness that should have resulted in such a deadly collapse.

INSPECTION OF THE MEDICAL KIT

The next day, upon returning to the dig site, I asked to see Dr. Grissard's medical kit. Mohammed had retrieved the key from the doctor's possessions and used it now to open the locker at the foot of Grissard's cot.

I was surprised to see the bottle of smelling salts in its rightful place among the other white bottles. "Someone must have returned it," I said. "Who else has a key to the locker?" "No one," answered Mohammed. "To my knowledge, there is only one key."

With considerable trepidation, I opened the bottle of smelling salts and gingerly sniffed. The pungent aroma of ammonia assaulted my nostrils. But nothing else. Mohammed sniffed it also. "Good salts," he said in his simple way, then capped it and returned it to its spot in the kit.

To review the most vital clues, see Deductive Reasoning on p. 126.

"THE TICKERTAPE SUICIDE"

CASPER GRANT'S SUICIDE NOTE

"Amalgamated Iron ended the day at 193. There's no possible hope. This is the best way for everyone. Tell June I love her. Casper."

EXAMINE CASPER GRANT'S BATHROOM

At first, Vaile noticed nothing strange. And then he saw it, a coffeelike stain discoloring the area around the drain of the porcelain sink. Miss Richardson said she had never noticed the stain before.

CHECK OUT TICKERTAPE MACHINES

Jimmy Fink, a broker on the fourth floor, admitted tossing the machine out. "The market's free fall was making me crazy.

Around 4:30, I cut the wire, opened the window, and chucked the blasted thing out. I didn't even look where it fell. My secretary can confirm all this. This morning, I was going to go into the alley to see if it was still in one piece, but a cop stopped me. What the heck's going on?"

To review the most vital clues, see Deductive Reasoning on p. 127.

"THE MAN IN CABIN 16"

CHECK THE CASUALTY LIST

The police captain reviewed the list. "According to the manifest, 96 souls were on board, 60 crew members and 36 passengers. We've retrieved all the bodies. Twenty-two crew bodies. We also found the remains of 13 passengers. The total number of survivors is 61." He added in his head. "Thirteen dead passengers plus 22 dead crew. Add that to the 61 survivors? Yep, that's 96. Everyone's accounted for."

INTERVIEW THE DOCTOR

The *Hindenburg*'s physician, Dr. Manfred Heil, escaped unscathed and had been at work examining the passenger bodies. He confided in Jack. "The man we saw in Cabin 16, he is not among the dead. We have checked identification on all the passengers. They're all accounted for. The corpse of Rudolph Lang seems to have disappeared."

OBSERVE TWO ATTENDANTS

Jack meandered through the large customs shed, his eyes peeled for the leather pouch. Fritzy sat on a metal suitcase, cradling what looked like a broken arm. Around the rest of his body was a bulky blanket. When the first ambulance arrived, Fritzy pushed to the front of the line, claiming to need immediate attention.

It took Jack some time to find Günther. The attendant was sitting on the floor in a corner, his uniform looking even more ill-fitting than it had during the flight. His mustache and mutton-chop sideburns had been badly singed and the poor, vain man was doing his best to hide this disfigurement.

To review the most vital clues, see Deductive Reasoning on p. 127.

"THE CORNER OF HOLLYWOOD & CRIME"

CORONER'S REPORT

The bruise on the left temporal lobe and the chlorinated water in the lungs are both consistent with drowning. In the stomach were substantial levels of barbiturates and alcohol. From the rate of dispersion, it is estimated that the deceased ingested both substances at least half an hour prior to death.

Due to the temperature of the bath water, it is impossible to determine the exact time of death.

GUARD AT THE GATE

"The servants had all gone home. No one was on the property when Miss Doral returned from the studio last night around seven.

"Mr. Doral arrived shortly after the quake. He was anxious to see if there was any damage. The sister, Brenda, showed up about an hour later. The only damage was the pool, not surprising since it was stuck out over the cliff. The water had all spilled out and down the hill.

"I let the press guys in at 11:45. Mr. McMasters bullied his way in about five minutes later. A few minutes after midnight, everyone left except Brenda and Dexter Doral. Those two had their own rooms and often spent the night. Nothing else happened until Miss Doral's secretary drove in a little before 6 A.M."

SEARCH THE BEDROOM

A Louis XIV boudoir decorated in white and beige. On a corner desk is a copy of the divorce papers, settling a lump sum of $50,000 on Ben McMasters. In the drawers are various investment certificates, a large stock portfolio, and partnership deeds in a real-estate holding company, all in the name of Marian Doral.

A walk-in closet contains an assortment of dresses, gowns, and shoes. A nearby table is strewn with a full array of Miss Doral's signature makeup collection, along with stands holding four wigs, each in a hairstyle made famous by the star.

To review the most vital clues, see Deductive Reasoning on p. 128.

To review the most vital clues, see Deductive Reasoning on p. 128.

"TWO SWORDSMEN OF VERONA"

EXAMINE THE BODY

Bertram called for torches and by their light made an examination of Lord Capulet's body. On unwrapping the bandage, he discovered a second, smaller wound, barely more than a deep needle prick, several inches lower on the abdomen than the fatal thrust.

EXAMINE THE SITE

Beside the body, Bertram discovered a single, wine-splashed glove and immediately recognized it as the property of Count Anselmo. Bertram recalled having seen the count remove his gloves during his inspection of the scene.

As the footmen removed Lord Capulet, Bertram noticed that the grass underneath the body was dry.

WHEREABOUTS OF THE CHARACTERS

Through judicious conversations with his betters, Bertram learned the following:

- After finding her husband asleep at 11 P.M., Lady Capulet retired to her chamber. Her maid confirms her presence there until the alarm was raised.

- Count Anselmo was alone in his own chambers until approximately 11, when he joined his cousin, Prince Escalus, for a tour of the castle grounds.

- Prince Escalus was with his steward until Count Anselmo came and suggested a walk of the grounds.

- Lord Montague was with his family until just before 11, when he left for his weekly visit to his son Romeo's crypt. He claimed to be there alone until after midnight.

To review the most vital clues, see Deductive Reasoning on p. 128.

DEDUCTIVE
REASONING

A Brief Review of the Most Vital Clues

"FALL OF A SOCIAL CLIMBER"

THE POISON, MODERATUS was sure, had been aconite, ground up from the yellow buttercups. Anyone in the house prior to the party had access to them, including Lady Sabbina, Achilius, and Norteo.

Moderatus thought back to his master's death. The hunting dog, now in the shallow grave, had been lapping up the spilled water, so the finger bowl must have been the source of the poison. Norteo, he recalled, had been in charge of filling the bowls. But one thing stood between the Nubian slave and a charge of murder, the actor Eppides. He had also been using this bowl, yet he had not been poisoned.

As Moderatus thought of the actor, a few oddities came to mind. Eppides certainly had no motive for killing his host, a relatively new acquaintance. But there had been greasy stains on his dinner robe. And among the toilet items that Norteo was returning to him, there had not been a razor. That seemed strange indeed.

"THE CHALICE OF CANA"

NO ONE HAD said a word about the lack of blood on Friar Germain's robe. But this detail intrigued Jean, whose uncle had been a butcher. From his own experience with animals, Jean knew that blood flows freely until the heart stops pumping.

The only logical explanation for the lack of blood was that Friar Germain had already been dead when he was stabbed. This theory was supported by the fact that, according to the Bishop, Germain had clutched his chest, far from the site of the dagger wound in the stomach.

The nearly dry circle of felt in the treasury also provided a clue. It meant that the chalice hadn't been removed until after the lightning strike. Rain must have fallen through the hole in the roof before the chalice was removed from its place on the red felt.

"Dead Man's Chest"

CAPTAIN WILL HAD been in the chest when he was stabbed, of this John was certain. He wasn't a trained physician, merely a sawbones surgeon. Still, the blood spatters on the inside walls could only have been made by the pumping heart of a living being.

The captain probably entered through the storeroom door. It opened onto an alley, away from the eyes of any neighbors. But who had opened it from the inside—Martha, or Rooster, or someone else?

The weapon itself, a dagger, would have been easily concealed. That, after all, is the main advantage of a dagger. But what about the mandrake root? Enough of the mysterious powder could kill, but the captain hadn't been poisoned. He'd been stabbed—while alive.

John couldn't help thinking of the captain's change of attitude in the past few days. Normally an even-tempered man, he had become dark and moody, one might even say suspicious.

"Death in the Serene Republic"

GIORGIO PRESTO, THE Doge's investigator, thought over the paltry evidence. Four things stood out.

The first was Lucrezia's body in the canal. Why hadn't it bobbed to the surface? The obvious response is that it had been caught on a submerged bar. But if this were true, why hadn't someone run into it before the fruit vendor?

The second discrepancy dealt with Lucrezia's costume. After the ball and after her death, she had Tomasso's gold mask. But the witness at the bridge described the mask as silver. Was the eyewitness mistaken?

Also, Lucrezia's stomach was empty, even though she had eaten at midnight, less than three hours earlier.

Finally, there was the matter of the indoor boat slip. According to Cesare, its current repair work is repeated yearly. Yet, according to a servant, the slip was repaired just three months ago.

"A Clockwork Murder"

HANS RECALLED SITTING in the Brown Bear, sucking the foam from his beer, at the moment the town clock struck ten. It must have been in working order then, without a human body clogging up its works. That would set the time of death between 10:00 and 10:25, the hour announced on the clock-tower face. If Jurgen had indeed died at 10:25, then Johann would be able to vouch for Hans's innocence and he for Johann's.

The other three denizens of the Brown Bear had all left in plenty of time to climb the stairs and club a man over the head. Would Marta Braun have had the strength to deliver such a blow? Perhaps, thought Hans. She was a sturdy girl and anger can give power to even the weakest.

Hans glanced again at the mangled body and a rush of anger welled up in his heart. Why had the killer pushed him into the cogs and gears? Judging from the head wound, Jurgen might already have been dead at the time. Who would want to do something so cruel to the town, damaging the clockworks, perhaps beyond repair? Could there be any good reason for such malevolence?

"A Snake in the Ash Pile"

WHEN DOC MAYNARD saw the snake box, he breathed a sigh of relief. Johnny, it seemed, was telling the truth, at least about the snakebite. A rattler had indeed bitten Jesse Blackburn, but probably with some human help.

The bottle of poison pushed down into the ash pile indicates that the poison was disposed of after Hector emptied the ashes— unless, of course, Hector is lying about when he threw them out.

Since Johnny was still in town doing errands, he couldn't
have been the one to push the poison bottle down into the
newly wetted ashes.

"FIRE & RAIN"

AS THEY LEFT the Johnson house, Judge Cramdon took side-
ways glances at the other two men. They were all suspects, he
realized. Who else could have come and gone in this burned-
out neighborhood without being seen?

He mulled over all the small inconsistencies. For instance,
he himself was the only one to clearly hear the two shots. And
then there was the broken glass on the library floor, as if a
bullet had been fired into the room from outside.

The newfangled spring lock on the front door might be the
latest thing in security, but it also served an unexpected function. It guaranteed that the killer, once outside, could not re-
enter the victim's house.

There was one other clue that all of them had seen—a clue,
the judge realized, that pointed directly at the killer.

"THE RIPPER'S LAST VICTIM"

INSPECTOR ABBERLINE SPREAD out the documents on his desk-
top—the post mortem report, the police records, and the lurid
account from the *East London Observer*. "What we have here,"
he told Sergeant Godley, "are two discrepancies and a seeming
impossibility."

Godley nodded sagely. He knew better than even to hazard
a guess.

Abberline pointed to the newspaper. "First off, the reporter
described the victim's arms as being outstretched while the
doctor said her hands were raised to her throat. That's worth
checking out. Second discrepancy: On the evening of

September 30, Danny Wainwright seems to have been two places at once; with Jilly near Mitre Square and in custody for public drunkenness. The seeming impossibility concerns the handprints around Jilly's throat. How could anyone have strangled her in that position?"

"THE ECCENTRIC ALCHEMIST"

ROLF BERGER WAS not a police inspector, but he had the common sense of an Austrian bureaucrat, which served him just as well. For example, the body was cold and beginning to smell, so he knew that Greenway had been dead for more than just a few hours.

Rolf also knew there was something wrong about Greenway himself. The American had arrived in Prague in disguise and stayed in cheap lodgings. Weeks later, he befriended Count Tyrs in Vienna and seemed to be rich enough to afford renting a private railway car. In addition, the victim's scent had permeated the forged statuettes, meaning they had been in his possession, probably for a period of time.

Berger also noted a discrepancy between Vaclav's account of when the matchbox was found and what the count had told him.

"CURSE OF THE PHARAOH"

DAYS LATER, MY thoughts returned to the mysterious deaths and I made these notes in my journal:

"The lack of cyanide in Dr. Grissard's stomach indicates that the poison hadn't been mixed with food. He had not been poisoned by the tainted figs. This conclusion is supported by the strong ammonia odor on the figs. Grissard would not have eaten them in that odoriferous state. So, I conclude, the figs were poisoned after Grissard's death.

"I must now go back in my memory and think about the smelling salts used twice on that fateful day. Even at the time, I felt uneasy about something, as if I were missing some simple, obvious fact."

"THE TICKERTAPE SUICIDE"

THE TIME-STAMP on the thrown tickertape machine sets the time of death before 4:28, when the fourth-floor broker tossed his machine out the window.

If this was murder, as seems likely, then someone else wrote the suicide note, using a pen with black ink. The note had either been written in advance, possibly with the victim's pen; or it was written after Grant's fall with another pen, since Grant's pen had gone with him out the window.

"THE MAN IN CABIN 16"

JACK THOUGHT BACK to the captain's meeting in the lounge. The junior attaché had counted 61 crew members (60 in the lounge plus the first mate at the controls). But according to the manifest, there were only 60.

Speaking of the crew...Jack turned to look at Günther, the old attendant. The *Hindenburg*, like all of Germany, it seemed, took pride in their snappy, perfectly fitting uniforms. Günther seemed to be an exception.

Dr. Heil passed through Jack's line of vision, and the young American's gaze followed the German physician. There was something about him, too, although Jack couldn't quite place it. Was it his looks? Something he'd said? Or perhaps something that someone else had said?

"THE CORNER OF HOLLYWOOD & CRIME"

THE DEPARTMENT HAD already labeled this an accident. But several oddities had caught Officer Westlake's eye and now, sitting over a soda at a drugstore counter, he mulled them over.

According to the papers, Ben McMasters had no financial motive for murder. Back when he was Marian's husband, he'd had plenty. But after midnight chimed and the marriage was dissolved, he was assured of his $50,000 payoff and nothing more. Then there was the chlorinated water in her lungs. Something about that didn't make sense either.

Officer Westlake checked the timetable. Marian had been home alone from 7:00 until approximately 9:00 when her brother arrived. Brenda arrived about an hour later. The reporters were on the estate at 11:45, with Ben arriving a few minutes later. No one else was seen coming or going until Harriet Brown drove in shortly before 6 A.M.

"TWO SWORDSMEN OF VERONA"

CAPTAIN BERTRAM LAY on the cot in his quarters, kept awake by the oddities of the evening's events. For one thing, there was the dry grass under Lord Capulet's body. If Lady Capulet last saw her husband in bed at 11, after the rains began, then how could the grass under his body be dry? Lady Capulet must have lied about her husband's presence in the sickroom. Lord Capulet's death occurred before 11 that night.

Did Lady Capulet conspire to give her husband an alibi at 11, after he had sneaked out of the sickroom? And what of Lord Capulet's rapier wound? It appeared to be of lethal seriousness. Wasn't she concerned about his health?

Bertram fell asleep musing on Count Anselmo's wine-stained glove. He must remember to return it tomorrow.

SOLUTIONS

SOLUTION TO "FALL OF
A SOCIAL CLIMBER"

(1) Eppides, the actor. (2) He poisoned the finger bowl. (3) Marcus Livius had discovered his secret, that he was actually a woman.

Moderatus didn't dare voice his theory without showing some proof, and he settled on a simple deception. "The actor Eppides may be able to help us," he told Achilius, his new master. "If you and I and a magistrate were to visit his quarters, unannounced…"

Achilius trusted his slave enough not to question him. Early the next morning they set out on the short carriage ride from their marble and stone neighborhood to the wood and brick houses that made up the rest of Rome. They found the actor's quarters in a modest apartment above a cheese shop. Moderatus asked the magistrate to force the door, and Achilius nodded his consent.

The result was better than Moderatus could have expected. For there, caught on her small palate of a bed, in the last cobwebs of sleep, was the woman who called herself Eppides, the actor.

With her secret exposed, it didn't take the magistrate long to extract her story. "I'm an actor," she said with unapologetic anger. "But the world doesn't allow women on the stage, except in cheap mimes played on street corners for tips. So I re-made myself as Eppides, renowned for his female roles. Back in Athens, I had friends to help. But here I depended on my wits. Since I could never go to the public baths, I accepted Marcus Livius's invitation as a chance to clean myself. But the fawning fool interrupted my bath and discovered my secret.

"During the preparations, no one saw me pick the buttercups and borrow a pestle. Then at dinner, instead of washing my hands in the bowl, I slipped in the poisonous powder. I never touched the bowl again, but he did. His hands went from the bowl to the food to his mouth. It didn't take long."

Moderatus and Achilius shared the carriage ride back, while the magistrate stayed behind with the prisoner. "I knew the poison was in the finger bowl," he told Achilius. "The grease on his expensive robe proved that he hadn't been using the bowl, and the lack of a razor among his possessions led me to suspect he might actually be a woman. That would certainly account for the rude, familiar way that your father treated him at dinner."

On the feast day of the household gods, both Moderatus and Norteo were given their freedom, their names carved on ivory discharge tickets. A year later, Emperor Caracalla granted Roman citizenship to all free men, and Moderatus was on the way up his own social ladder.

SOLUTION TO "THE CHALICE OF CANA"

(1) Young Louis the stonecutter, after Germain died of a heart attack.
(2) He climbed down through the roof. (3) To steal the chalice.

Bishop Faisant ordained a day of repentance. No work would be done, just prayers offered up for the cathedral and for the return of the Lord's chalice. After a morning mass in the open square, Jean strolled down Cutters Lane, the makeshift village where the stonecutters would live for the next year or for the next twenty, however long it took or how long the chapter's money lasted.

He found Louis alone in his shack. The young man said no word of greeting but sat staring through the open doorway. Jean sat beside him and whispered.

"You saw Friar Germain dead inside the treasury, just as you called down to us. The poor man's heart must have failed him. That's not hard to imagine, given the lightning and the fire."

Louis said nothing.

"While the Bishop's men were busy breaking down the door, you returned to the hole in the roof. No one could see you climbing down and taking the chalice. You stabbed the dead body so we would think what we thought, that Friar Germain had been killed and the chalice stolen earlier. Did you leave the chalice on the roof?"

The stonecutter's voice was thick and soft. "I bundled it in my robe. Between my legs. It is undamaged. But even if I return it, they will kill me."

This was true. Every crime of any consequence was punishable by death. But crimes against the church demanded death by torture. Jean did not want to have his cathedral associated with such a scandal and execution.

When the chalice magically reappeared the next day, Bishop Faisant declared it a miracle and ordained a feast of celebration.

SOLUTION TO "DEAD MAN'S CHEST"

---

(1) Bart Pyle, the captain's mate. (2) He convinced Will to hide in the chest where he stabbed him. (3) Pyle wanted to be the new captain.

The surgeon had been trying to catch Pyle, the new captain, alone. He finally saw him napping on a wooded bluff overlooking the bay. A short while later, after a quick trip into town, John himself was climbing up the bluff for a private talk.

"I know you killed him," he told Bart Pyle, without any preamble.

The wily pirate looked shocked and vehemently denied any such thing.

"I know the whole story," John continued. "You poisoned the captain's mind by telling him the men were planning a mutiny. That's why he was acting so oddly. You told him to hide in the tavern and you would get the mutineers talking, so he could hear for himself. And that's what happened. But first you put mandrake powder in his rum.

"When Captain Will left the tavern, he came around to the storeroom door. You sneaked him in and helped him hide in the chest. A short while later, after he'd passed out from the powder, you returned to the storeroom. It was simple enough for you to open the chest and stab him. Then you brought us out another keg of ale."

Bart Pyle laughed. "You are a clever lad. I knew they'd blame it on Rooster, since there was so much bad blood between 'em. It's your ill fortune that you can't prove your story."

But John didn't have to prove it. On his trip into Port Royal, he had found the beadle of the court and coerced him into climbing the bluff and secreting himself behind a mass of sea grape. The official had heard everything.

SOLUTION TO "DEATH IN THE SERENE REPUBLIC"

(1) Cesare Contini and Maria Garda. (2) Maria impersonated her on the bridge. Lucrezia was killed elsewhere. (3) Cesare Contini's marital freedom and inheritance.

The killers had worked out a careful plan. Maria's rendezvous that night wasn't with Cesare but with the unwitting Lucrezia. Maria waited in the shadows by the Contini palazzo. When Lucrezia went inside her home, Maria took her place on the streets, dressed identically except for the mask, a last-minute change that Maria was unaware of.

Maria staged the suicide, jumping off the bridge and swimming to a deserted spot where she had planted a change of clothing. Meanwhile, back at his empty palazzo, Cesare drowned his wife. He closed off the boat slip and hid her body underwater until he and Maria could safely plant the corpse in the canal.

When Giorgio realized the importance of the gold mask, he called in Cesare and Maria for questioning. As before, Maria stayed calm while crossing the Bridge of Sighs. Cesare, however, broke down. Within an hour, Giorgio had a confession.

SOLUTION TO "A CLOCKWORK MURDER"

(1) Johann Sensenig. (2) He set the clock hand forward to give himself an alibi. (3) The grease stain on his sleeve.

Johann took a good, close look at the clockmaker's mangled body, then climbed back up through the cogs. "Your clothes are now all covered in grease," Hans said to the young herdsman. "If I'd only thought faster, I would have stopped you from climbing down."

Johann examined the grease marks on his *brezon* and trousers. "Ruined. My mother would tan my hide, except that I'm too old for such punishment."

"You're not too old for some punishments," Hans said darkly. "Why did you kill Carl Jurgen?"

Johann didn't bother to deny it. "It's true. I followed Marta here. From the bottom of the stairs I heard them. After Marta left, I came up here. And I killed him."

"You threw the body into the mechanism in order to stop the clock."

"That's right," Johann admitted with a casual shrug. "I unlocked the clock-face window, reached out, and moved the hands forward to 10:25. Then at 10:25, I made sure I was at the inn. How did you know, Hans? Was it that I didn't relock the window?"

"No," Hans answered. "I should have stopped you from going down into the gears. Then I would have had proof. I could have pointed to the grease on your *brezon*. The only way you could have acquired that stain would be from something up here, like the greasy hands of the clock."

"But now I'm covered with grease," Johann said with a smile. "Your proof is just one stain among many."

Hans paused to consider, and then returned the smile. "Ah, well. Perhaps now we can start over and hire us a competent clockmaker."

SOLUTION TO
"A SNAKE IN THE ASH PILE"

(1) Mabel Blackburn. (2) By nicotine, inserted into the wound at Doc Maynard's. (3) She was the only person who could have planted the bottle in the ash pile.

Doc Maynard was at his desk, writing a letter to his wife back in Georgia when Mabel Blackburn walked in without knocking. "Is it true?" she asked. "Hector says they found the poison Johnny used to kill Jesse."

"No." Doc put down his letter. "They found the poison you used to kill Jesse."

He couldn't really blame her. Jesse was a mean drunk who took most of Mabel's pie money. Her plan had been to let a rattlesnake loose in the cabin one morning when Jesse was still drunk. It worked. The snake bit. But thanks to Johnny's quick thinking, it looked as though he might recover.

Mabel was prepared with a back-up plan. During her few moments alone with Jesse, she brought out her bottle of nicotine and dabbed it into the wound. Anyone would think he'd died from the snake bite. Anyone but Doc Maynard.

Mabel looked him straight in the eye. "How did you know?"

"The nicotine is fast-acting. That means it was used while Jesse was here at my house. That eliminates Hector. As for Johnny or Abner, neither one could have buried the nicotine in the ashes. They were together the whole time. You were the only one who could have poisoned him and dumped the bottle."

Mabel nodded. "I didn't mean to frame anyone. I didn't think they would find the nicotine. But when they did..." She sighed. "I'm still glad he's dead."

SOLUTION TO "FIRE & RAIN"

---

(1) Judge Elmer Cramdon. (2) He killed Rory Johnson before arriving home, then fired the gun out his own window. (3) Judge Cramdon's umbrella in the victim's hall.

"I may have actually gotten away with it," the judge thought as he and Vera walked back toward their house.

That afternoon, he had gone straight from the Common Council to a meeting at Rory Johnson's home. The editor confronted the judge with his crime—taking bribes to ignore building-code violations, a practice that, the judge had to admit, contributed to the fire's deadly destruction.

He rebutted the accusation with a heavy candlestick and took the incriminating papers. On leaving Rory's house, he accidentally left his wet, monogrammed umbrella in the hall stand. The umbrella was damning evidence, proof that he'd been to Rory's house during the recent rainstorm. He had to get back in there and retrieve it. But how?

From the privacy of his study, the judge took his own revolver, removed one bullet, then shot out his open window straight through Rory's window. He had to claim he'd heard two shots. One bullet was sure to be found in the room and the judge had to preserve the illusion that Rory fired the shot through the window.

Upon "discovering" the body, the judge took the gun from his pocket and slipped it into Rory's hand. Unfortunately, it had to be the wrong hand, the hand facing the wall, his left hand. But no one had made a fuss about that. Elmer Cramdon was feeling pretty good.

"Elmer, where did you get that?" Vera had stopped and was looking at the umbrella in his hand. "I thought you left it…" And then her eyes went wide with surprise.

SOLUTION TO
"THE RIPPER'S LAST VICTIM"

(1) Danny Wainwright. (2) Danny and Jilly faked her attack. Danny strangled her while the reporter went for help. (3) As her husband, Danny inherited.

Jilly had fabricated her encounter with Jack the Ripper in order to profit from the publicity. Danny was in on the scheme and came up with a plan to extend her moment of fame. Jilly would now pretend to be an actual Ripper victim, a lucky and courageous survivor. But Danny, eyeing his wife's money and house, decided to change plans.

After her stint at the music hall, Jilly rushed to George Yard, their prearranged site. Danny brought the reporter from the other direction, speaking loudly enough to alert her. Once Danny was left alone with Jilly, kneeling above her head, he simply reached down and strangled her. By the time the reporter returned with the police, she was really dead.

Mary Kelly, the woman murdered shortly before Jilly, would be the last confirmed Ripper victim. The Autumn of Terror of 1888 ended suddenly, with no explanation and no arrest.

SOLUTION TO
"THE ECCENTRIC ALCHEMIST"

(1) Count Tyrs. (2) To recover the stolen figurines. (3) Tyrs lied about when the matchbox had been found.

Count Tyrs might have been a bit of a swindler, but Herbert Greenway was the real thing. He arrived in Prague, heard about the Tyrs figurines and spent the first weeks of his stay having forgeries made. Masquerading as an enthusiastic investor was a sure way to gain the count's trust and gain access to his manor house.

After replacing the figurines with fakes, Greenway engineered his own disappearance. But before Greenway could don a disguise and leave Prague, Vaclav found the matchbox. By this time, the count had discovered the theft. He gave Vaclav the night off, then drove himself to the Hotel Club where he killed Greenway and recovered his figurines. Back at the manor house, Count Tyrs replaced the originals and buried the forgeries.

Rolf became suspicious when he compared Vaclav's claim—that the matchbook had been found the day after Greenway's disappearance—to Count Tyrs's claim—that it had been found a day later.

SOLUTION TO "CURSE OF THE PHARAOH"

---

(1) Dr. Grissard, by accident. (2) With the poisoned smelling salts he'd used on Effendi. (3) To prevent Effendi from exposing his smuggling.

One of the most puzzling questions I faced was: How did the bottle of smelling salts get from Dr. Grissard's death scene back inside the medical kit in his footlocker? The answer, of course, was, it didn't. There were two bottles of smelling salts, the white, untainted bottle and the brown one containing the cyanide.

Once this fact made its way into my consciousness, the solution was clear.

Dr. Grissard had been robbing artifacts from the tomb and hiding them in the tunnel. He rigged a booby trap to fall on any unlucky intruder, and the tunnel collapsed on the snooping Effendi.

But Effendi didn't die. Grissard realized he might survive and expose the theft. So, when Mohammed handed Grissard the smelling salts, Grissard did a sleight of hand, substituting his own brown bottle of poisoned salts.

How did the doctor happen to have a bottle of poisoned salts on his person? That I will never know. But there is no other possible explanation. He was handed a white bottle, but a brown bottle came out of his jacket pocket.

After Effendi's death, the doctor placed the poisoned salts in his pocket. He returned the white bottle to the kit, locking it in his footlocker. It was a perfect murder. But Grissard had no way of foretelling his upcoming accident, no way of knowing that Mustaf would unwittingly use the poisoned bottle on him.

Seconds after Dr. Grissard's death, Mustaf smelled the air and realized what must have happened. Afraid of being arrested, Mustaf poured the rest of the deadly smelling salts onto the figs, hoping people would think Grissard had been poisoned this way.

Suspicion naturally fell on Mustaf, but there was no proof, and as the legend of the curse grew, the authorities were more than willing to credit the supernatural for both deaths.

I did nothing to dissuade them from this conclusion. Perhaps I should have, but I saw no reason to sully reputations and, more, imperil the integrity of my camp. In a way, I suppose I'm as responsible as anyone for the superstition of the pharaoh's curse.

SOLUTION TO
"THE TICKERTAPE SUICIDE"

(1) Grant's suicide note quotes the closing price of Amalgamated Iron. (2) Lawrence Baxter. (3) Brown ink from Baxter's fountain pen caused the stain in the sink.

If the tickertape machines were running two hours late, and Grant had received no phone calls or talked to anyone, then he couldn't have known a stock's closing price until 5:30, long after his death. So, the suicide note was a fake.

Sergeant Vaile reconstructed the murder. Fear and anger were running high on Black Tuesday. Threats and arguments and tears flew up and down Wall Street like leaves in the wind. Someone entered Grant's office. There was an argument.

Vaile knew that Grant had been knocked unconscious

before being pushed out the window. Otherwise, someone would have heard a scream.

The killer, coming to his senses, figured that a short, anguished note would help establish a suicide. But Grant's pen had gone out the window with him. To make the note look convincing, the killer had to use black ink. So, he emptied his own fountain pen into the sink and refilled it from Grant's inkwell.

The brown stain in the sink points directly to Lawrence Baxter.

SOLUTION TO "THE MAN IN CABIN 16"

---

(1) Rudolph Lang didn't die. (2) Dr. Heil. (3) Günther, the attendant, who is Rudolph Lang in disguise.

Jack did a little addition. The number of souls accounted for, survivors and victims, was 96, the same as on the airship's manifest. But after the explosion, there seemed to be one more crew member and one less passenger. "No wonder I hadn't seen Günther before," he muttered. "And no wonder his uniform didn't fit."

Jack showed his credentials to the police captain and explained his predicament. "I have no authorization to take that courier pouch. But the security of the United States..."

Within five minutes, Jack had the pouch and was in a taxi on his way to the train station and Washington, D.C. It all made sense now. Lang needed to throw Jack off his trail. His solution was to fake his own death and then sneak off the *Hindenburg* disguised as a crew member. When he saw Jack walking by his cabin window, Lang went into his act, crying out and groaning. Dr. Heil was nearby, observing, making sure that he would be the only person to examine Lang and pronounce him dead.

Heil supplied Lang with a uniform. Sideburns and a showy waxed mustache completed the disguise. The other crew members, all loyal Germans, were instructed to treat Lang as a regular cabin attendant.

"I should have known as soon as I heard the doctor's name," Jack chided himself. When Lang spoke to his secret confidant in the lounge, he seemed to find amusement in saying "heil." Lang had been making a pun. The man in the lounge was Dr. Heil.

SOLUTION TO "THE CORNER OF HOLLYWOOD & CRIME"

---

(1) Drowned accidentally in the swimming pool. (2) Dexter and Brenda, by masquerading as Marian for the press conference. (3) Inheritance.

Thirty years later, while watching an old Marian Doral movie on TV, retired officer Marvin Westlake would tell his grandkids this story. He had never told it to the detectives who spent ten minutes investigating the accident, nor to the tabloids who would have paid him well for it. A crime had been committed, but in Westlake's mind it wasn't a serious crime.

The key for him was the chlorinated water in Marian Doral's lungs. The estate's only chlorinated water was in the pool, which had been emptied by the 8:37 P.M. quake. Therefore, Marian Doral drowned in the pool before, or perhaps even during, the earthquake.

So, if she was dead before midnight, who appeared on the balcony and talked to the reporters? It had to be Brenda Doral, using her sister's heels, makeup, clothing, and wig to masquerade as the dead star. When Ben McMasters came too close to the stairs, Brenda retreated into the bedroom, changed costumes, and re-emerged as herself.

And the motive? If Dexter and Brenda could postpone Marian's perceived time of death until after midnight, then Ben would no longer have claim on the estate and the inheritance could pass to Marian's next of kin, her brother and sister.

SOLUTION TO "TWO SWORDSMEN OF VERONA"

(1) Lord and Lady Capulet, who were conspiring to murder Lord Montague. (2) Count Anselmo. (3) The wine-stained glove.

Captain Bertram awoke the next morning, eyes focused on the wine-stained glove on the stool beside his cot. The answer was there, as simple as the daylight itself.

During their duel, Lord Montague inflicted a minor wound, barely piercing his opponent's leather jerkin. Lord Capulet then faked his injury, hoping to provoke the prince into banishing Montague.

When Prince Escalus didn't exile anyone, Capulet revised his plan. With his wife acting as doctor and alibi, Capulet sneaked out and went in search of Montague, who would be keeping his regular appointment at Romeo's crypt. On his way, Capulet ran into Anselmo who immediately guessed at the truth. Incensed by this treachery, Anselmo killed Capulet. Afraid of being banished, Anselmo moved the body to its position under the window and, in the process, lost a glove. Not knowing what had happened to it, Anselmo retrieved another pair before joining Prince Escalus for their stroll.

The wine-stained glove was the key. Bertram realized that it must have been on the ground before he spilled the wine. If Anselmo had dropped the glove later, there would be no stain. The wine would have already seeped into the wet ground.

INDEX

Gathering Evidence and Deductive Reasoning pages for individual stories are in italics.

Hy Conrad is an Edgar-nominated mystery writer, who began his career as a New York playwright. He was one of the first authors to become involved in the world of interactive fiction, developing and writing such projects as The MysteryDiscs, Clue VCR, and the Internet mystery serial, *Abel Adventures*.

Mr. Conrad has developed numerous games, mystery and otherwise, for Parker Brothers and Milton-Bradley, as well as computer-based mysteries. In the late 1990s, he was the creative director of Mysterynet, the largest Web site devoted to the mystery genre.

He has been a writer and story editor of the television detective series *Monk* since its premiere in 2002. This is Hy Conrad's eighth book of short mysteries for Sterling Publishing.

His collections of mysteries have been translated into Spanish, French, Portuguese, Russian, Swedish, Norwegian, Finnish, Hungarian, Japanese, Chinese, and Korean.